The Billionaire's Elusive Lover

Elizabeth Lennox

Table of Contents

Chapter 1

"Thank you so much Edna," Helen Miller enthused, shaking the older woman's hand. "I promise I'll be out of here quickly."

Edna chuckled. "Don't worry. My boss isn't scheduled to be back for hours. He won't know a thing."

Edna looked at the beautiful woman with the black hair that curled down her back in what could only be described as riotous. "What are you trying to capture?" she asked, fascinated at the way the young woman was examining the sky and the windows, as if they held the secret to the world and she was determined to find the key. Edna had never seen such passion, she thought silently. The idea of maintaining that much energy all the time seemed exhausting to Edna.

Helen smiled back at Edna. "The sunset today is going to be perfect," she enthused. "The afternoon heat has created a heavy haze that will filter the sunshine. I guarantee the colors will be spectacular." She smiled over at the other woman, an excited glint in her eyes. "Just wait and you'll see."

Edna smiled at the young woman. She couldn't believe she'd let this woman into Alec Dionysius' office but there was just something about her that had Edna violating sacred rules. Maybe it was her energy or enthusiasm, or something even more subtle that had her convinced that everything would be okay.

Normally, no one got through to this office without an appointment and usually those appointments were booked months in advance. Mr. Dionysius was a very busy and extremely powerful man and everyone wanted to have "just five minutes" of his time. His security team always surrounded him when he was out and about in public or even at private parties. But up here, in this office, it was Edna that was the obstacle. No one got through her unless Mr. Dionysius allowed it.

1

Which made this aberration all the more strange. She watched as the lovely woman clicked her camera over and over again, fascinated by her facial expressions. When she pulled out another camera, Edna considered asking her questions, but then stopped herself, seeing the intense concentration on the younger woman's face.

Ten minutes later, Helen snapped the last shot and dropped her camera into her padded, canvas bag. "See what I mean?" she said almost breathlessly, staring out at the horizon.

Edna stopped her curious inspection of the brunette beauty and looked out the floor to ceiling windows in her boss' office. At her first glimpse, she gasped in surprise. "Oh, my!" she said, her hand covering her throat as she looked at the spectacular array of colors shimmering across the horizon. In a reverent whisper, Edna agreed, "You were right, Helen. This view is amazing!"

The two women stood there for a long moment, their eyes glued to the horizon as they continued to watch the changing colors of the sunset. Neither were aware of the executive floor security guard or the clerical support woman who worked for Edna as they both walked into the sacred domain of the man in charge. All four of them stood still, awe-struck by the light show. The silence was complete, broken only by the flashes of color slowly forming a silent, colorful melody as they shifted across the evening sky. The kaleidoscopic of light from the setting sun had an almost symphonic beauty to it against which, even a heavy breath would be a violation.

"What the hell is going on in here?" a deep voice demanded harshly from the doorway.

Four people jumped at the exact same moment. Edna spun around, her shoulders instantly tense and wary. "Oh, Mr. Dionysius! You're back early!" Briefly, Edna gripped the desk for support, then pulled herself together. Straightening her shoulders, she looked around at the others, then focused her gaze direction on the man who was still glaring a the four people that had violated the sanctity of his off. "I'm so sorry!" she announced, folding her hands in front of her.

"That's not very informative," he replied with dry sarcasm.

Helen tried to look away. She really did. She didn't want to be fascinated by a man who would interrupt such an incredible moment in time and not appreciate its beauty. Unfortunately, her eyes were glued to the most amazing male she'd ever seen. He was tall with a chiseled jaw, hawk-like nose and black, dangerous eyes. His perfectly tailored suit framed his body with an elegant façade but she was still able to see the broad shoulders and flat stomach which distinguished the latent menace underneath the tailored fabric. His hands were aggressively resting on his hips, pushing back the suit jacket to reveal power more suited to a furious male lion than a mere human male.

The fact that he was glaring at her didn't register in her mind for a long moment until her gaze finally came to rest back on his face after surveying the rest of him with a slow, compulsive perusal. The heat that flared within her stomach almost made her knees give out. His eyes captured hers, held her captive and she felt powerless, completely at his mercy. No man had ever made her feel this helpless. Nor had any man ever made her feel anything like this. Her stomach felt like it was filled with bubbles that were floating, popping and moving into her bloodstream to zing around her body. Her mind told her to leave but her feet were immobile as she continued to take in the man with all of his incredible strength.

Helen heard her new friend's attempt at conciliating the angry man and Helen wished she could step in and offer her apology, protect Edna from the man's wrath, but she was still held captive by his eyes.

Edna stepped forward, almost as if she were trying to protect the other occupants. Out of the corner of her eye, Helen noticed the clerical staff member slink out of the office, unnoticed by the glaring male. But Edna stood firm, refusing to skulk away as well. Mick, the security guard, stood firm, his jaw clenching as he stepped forward, ready to take the blame. But Edna lifted her hand and Mick reluctantly stopped.

With a mild gesture behind her, Edna offered a weak explanation. "I...um...I was just letting Ms. Miller...she wanted to..." Edna fumbled through the excuse but she was too nervous to finish it.

Realizing that Edna was trying to protect finally allowed Helen to break free from the tall man's hold on her logic.

"Mr...." she fumbled because she wasn't sure who he was but wouldn't let her new friends down in this situation. They'd gone out of their way to help her and she didn't want to repay their kindness by dumping them to the wolves. Or wolf, she corrected. This man was definitely baring his teeth. With a huff, she glared right back up at the tall, formidable man. "I'm sorry that I don't know your name but this is all my fault." She gestured to Mick and Edna, then focused back on the arrogant jerk. "I asked Mick to introduce me to Edna who allowed me into your office. I just wanted a picture," she explained, lifting her camera bag, "and she's stood with me the whole time to make sure I didn't do anything besides take pictures so if there's anything confidential in this office, I promise I didn't see it."

Obviously, her explanation didn't do the trick because the anger in his eyes didn't ease. "And you think that's okay?" he commented with an affectation of calm, moving slowly across the room, his eyes never leaving her face. "What, exactly, were you photographing?" he asked.

Good! An easy question. She needed those right now since her knees were trembling at his closer proximity. "The sunset," Helen replied with an uptick of her chin. She poked her thumb in the general vicinity of the large window behind her. "A combination of the storm and the intense heat we had earlier today, the refracting light was particularly extraordinary tonight. I really didn't mean to invade your space in this way. I promise I'll get out of your way now." Helen adjusted her camera bag over her shoulder with shaking fingers, pulling it higher onto her shoulder and quickly walked toward the double doors that would give her freedom from the strange power he seemed to have over her.

"Stop," he ordered in a deep, commanding voice when she started to move past him. Turning to the others, he dismissed them with a silent glare. They immediately got the message and left the office as quickly as possible.

Helen watched her friends leave, knowing they still felt as if they were in trouble. She hated thinking that her actions had caused them harm and turned to face the person who had made them feel uncomfortable, allowing all her confused emotions toward this man to coalesce into anger, which was much easier to define and handle than the ambiguous feelings that had been spiraling through her system moments ago. She didn't understand those feelings. She understood, and could react to, this burgeoning anger that filled her with a righteous fury, all directed towards this tall, formidable man who thought he could speak to people in such a demoralizing manner.

"That was very rude of you," Helen snapped, her eyes coming back to him, unafraid of showing her irritation.

Alec's eyes snapped back to the brunette beauty but he didn't say a word. He waited until he heard the door close behind them before speaking. "Excuse me?" he replied with lethal calm. Anyone else would know that he'd just been pushed beyond what he considered acceptable but this tiny woman seemed oblivious to the possible consequences of his anger.

Despite the wariness in her eyes, the terrified woman straightened her shoulders and faced him head on, causing a spurt of admiration to hit him.

"I said, you were very rude to your staff. You should apologize. It's my fault that they let me in here so you should only be mad at me. There was no need for you to show your impatience at them."

Alec couldn't believe his ears. Was he actually being taken to task by a woman who barely reached his shoulders? His eyes traveled up and down her figure once again and he couldn't deny that he was intrigued. No, he corrected. He'd been intrigued when he'd walked in and caught sight of her gorgeous hair that fell down her back and witnessed her cute little bottom wiggling against her gauzy skirt.

Now that she was standing here, challenging him and telling him off, so to speak, he was more than intrigued. He was fascinated. Alec acknowledged that a large part of his fascination came also from her voluptuous curves that were barely encased in the tight, green tee-shirt and the stunning dark green eyes that were glaring back at him. Her mouth was spouting commands and issuing statements he wouldn't allow from any of his staff under any circumstances. In a split second decision, he also knew in that moment that he would soon have those lips whispering softer words into his ear in the very near future.

He kept his face impassive as he moved closer to her, explaining in the most reasonable tones that she was currently in a great deal of danger. "It is their responsibility to make sure no one enters this office without my approval. You standing here is evidence that they were not doing their job very well. What makes you think that I should apologize for mediocre performance?"

Her sexy mouth dropped open at his statement that his staff members had been slack in their vigilance simply because she'd used his office for a few short minutes.

"That's ridiculous," the beauty snapped up at him, taking a step back.

She was a tiny thing, he realized. But the disparities in their individual height didn't cause her to back down. She had to tilt her head back to look up at him, but that only allowed him to see the sparks shooting from those beautiful, Green eyes.

He could see that he was having an impact on her senses as well. Being this close, he could see the fluttering pulse at the base of her throat. Yes, my dear woman, he thought with relish. You are correct; you are in very grave danger!

Helen glared up at him, wishing that she could...what? What could she do to the tall, dangerous man? He was too close, she thought. And his proximity definitely wasn't good for her concentration. Unfortunately, Helen couldn't come up with a good plan to take the man's arrogance down a notch. Instead, her traitorous mind was contemplating what he had underneath that perfect white shirt, wondering if he had muscles or if he was just well made. She should be trying to figure out a way to protect Edna and Mick and not wondering about the man's muscles!

Concentrate, she told herself sternly. What happened in the next few minutes could mean the difference between two people having a job tomorrow or being sacked immediately.

Taking in a slow, calming breath...that didn't calm her in the least, she looked up at him and tried for a conciliatory tone. "They were just being nice," she stated, hoping that her voice was more neutral than she felt.

Unfortunately, his lips thinned slightly at her response. "I don't pay them to be nice," he replied with a voice that suggested she shouldn't argue any longer.

Helen couldn't believe anyone could be so handsome and yet at the same time, so lethal. She wouldn't admit that she was scared and squared her shoulders, wishing she could find the right words to help out Edna and Mick. Deciding that caution was the better part of valor, she decided to take this argument down a notch. "Well, they were very nice and helped me out a lot tonight. I got some wonderful pictures of the sunset so..." she side stepped around him warily, maintaining eye contact, just as one would with a wild, dangerous animal. Still, she lowered her voice another notch, trying to appease his anger. "I'll just get out of your hair if you'll promise me that you won't be mean to them about this situation."

Quick as a flash, the man's arm reached out and imprisoned her, pinning her between his long, muscular arm and the hard wall behind her, effectively halting her retreat. He stared at her for a long moment, and she suspected that he was trying to figure out how to make her follow his orders.

Stiffening her shoulders, she glared right back up at him, silently warning him that she wasn't going to back down. He must have seen the sincerity and confidence on her face, because the man laughed.

"You're joking, right?" he asked, his dark eyes changing. The anger disappeared, but Helen was pretty sure that the...interest?...was even more dangerous than the anger from moments before.

Since she was trapped on the right by his arm blocking her exit, she once again tried to move deftly to the left in order to put just a little space between them. His close proximity wasn't good for her. Unfortunately, he must have anticipated her move, because his body shifted so suddenly, and so subtly, she didn't know how, but she was suddenly trapped once again by his body and the luxurious sofa.

Helen shook her head, her long gold hoops brushing against her cheek. "Absolutely not. If you're going to be mad at someone, then be mad at me. Call the police and have me arrested for trespassing if you'd like but leave them out of this."

He leaned forward, his broad chest pressing her legs back against the back of the sofa, all anger vanishing at her astonishing demand. Once again, Helen suspected that the new emotion was more terrifying. And more dangerous!

"So you used my office to take pictures. I'm guessing you're a professional photographer, correct?"

Helen was stunned by the sudden change in him. His eyes were no longer glaring at her angrily. In fact, she thought she saw a small smile curl his lips. But that was ridiculous, she told herself quickly. No one could change emotions that fast.

"Yes," she replied, pulling her heavy camera bag closer defensively. His anger she could deal with. This new challenge was different, and oh so much more intimidating. She didn't understand why her heart was beating frantically and her breath seemed to be caught in her throat. She leaned back, wishing she could be more confident and face the challenge he was silently issuing but, for some reason, she was terrified of the new threat.

"I'm a freelance photographer." She swallowed hard and licked her dry lips.

His focus shifted to the movement of her tongue. Could he sense the increased pulse at the base of her long, sexy neck? Helen suspected that he had. Not a lot was missed by this man's observant gaze.

"So you owe me, as far as I can see."

Helen blinked in confusion. "I owe you?" she gasped. "How so?"

She couldn't suppress the shiver that sparked through her, or the blush that stained her cheeks.

"You are here in my building, using my office to take pictures which you're then going to turn around and sell to someone else, probably a magazine or some sort of collection, correct?" he stated.

His questions suddenly made sense and for a moment, she was suddenly extremely disappointed that this conversation had turned to profit. She shrugged as if she did this kind of negotiation all the time.

"You want a portion of the profits from the pictures, is that it?" she asked, her heart falling to her stomach because she wouldn't get much for the pictures and every penny counted when one was a photographer.

His eyes didn't reveal any hint of his next words so they took Helen by surprise. "No. You owe me dinner," he stated firmly. Deftly, the man plucked her bag from her shoulder and started walking away.

Helen gasped, completely off kilter with his unexpected demand, and thrown utterly for a loop by his action. "What are you doing with my cameras?" she almost yelled, chasing after him as he started to leave his office. "Give them back!"

"I'm not taking them from you," Alex assured her, turning so suddenly that she plowed into him. His arm immediately went around her waist to hold her steady, her small frame trapped against his taller one and he instantly liked the feeling.

He saw her mouth open in surprise and his mind had to work hard to control his body. He wanted this woman. And if his body had anything to say about it, it would have to be soon. "I'm simply carrying them for you until we reach my car. This bag is heavy."

Alex wanted to move his arm, to explore her curves. But the woman was skittish enough already. He'd have to back down, to treat her with caution. She was a fascinating combination of fire and fear, of innocence and determination.

Women often came into his life, their intentions clear. He'd enjoyed their offerings in the past, but those women knew the score. His relationships had been transactional with his previous lovers.

But looking at this woman, Helen, he knew that he she would be different.

How different, he wasn't quite sure. However, Alec knew that he was going to find out. No matter what, this woman fascinated him more than any other woman ever had.

Helen struggled to form a thought. Her mind was spinning as his arm tightened around her for a brief moment, then relaxed. Her fingers itched to touch him, to further investigate the hard muscles that her body was currently feeling. Her hands touched his arms to steady herself and her eyes followed, fascinated by the muscles underneath the smooth Egyptian cotton of his shirt. He was amazingly strong, she thought absently.

A flexing of those muscles distracted her for a moment. She looked up into his eyes, startled by the man as well as by her unprecedented captivation.

But just as quickly, she realized what she was doing and her mind clicked back, refocusing on the issue at hand and dismissing her enthrallment with his body.

Shaking her head, she pressed against his arms, needing space. "I can't go to dinner with you." Thankfully, he released her and Helen quickly dropped her hands down to her sides and prayed she wouldn't fall down.

"Why not?" he asked. She felt his eyes move over her, pausing on her breasts that were heaving softly with her efforts to control her desire to reach out and touch him once more.

When her eyes lifted from those impressive shoulders, she realized that he was waiting expectantly. Right! He'd asked a question. Dinner? Right! Why couldn't she eat dinner with him!

"Um....because...." she couldn't think when he was this close. She needed to put additional space between them but her arms and legs weren't following the direction from her brain. "Because," she said once again but this time, it came out only as a whisper.

"Not a good enough excuse," he replied softly, his voice husky.

He stepped back again, knowing that she needed a bit of space. He did too! And Alec was astonished by that fact.

Still, he understood that his close proximity might scare her. He'd only met the woman fifteen minutes ago and all he could think about was getting her into his bed. From the wariness he was seeing in those lovely, green eyes, he would have to take things a bit slower than he'd like.

However, he truly wanted to understand this woman. With that intention in mind, he turned and walked out of his office, aware of the slender beauty following quickly on his heels.

"Edna, call The Westin and get a table for two in...," he glanced at his watch, "twenty minutes," he said to the still nervous Edna as he passed by her desk.

Helen wasn't just interesting, she was cute! His interest was deeper and went well beyond sexual. Although, Alec didn't discount his desire!

Helen raced along behind him, her mouth dropping open at the mention of the very exclusive restaurant located in the heart of the financial district of London.

Now that she had some breathing room, her anger was able to diffuse the more mystifying feelings she'd been experiencing. Plus, his renewed arrogance sparked her anger, a must safer emotion. It was cleansing and helped her regain her focus.

"Don't be ridiculous, Mr. Dionysius. Edna can't get a table at the Weston on such short a notice," she snapped, instantly defending the woman who had helped her earlier. "That's impossible."

In response, Alec turned back to look down at the lovely and enticing brunette, his dark eyes holding her green ones hostage. He didn't say a word but simply waited, listening for Edna's voice. He smiled wolfishly as his secretary calmly informed the maitre'd of the Westin that

Alec and a guest would be arriving shortly.

"Thank you very much, Jeffrey," Edna replied, smiling at whatever the man said to her in response.

Placing the receiver back in it's cradle, she smiled at Helen. "The table will be waiting for you when you arrive," she stated efficiently.

Stunned, Helen shook her head in amazement. "How is that possible? You need reservations so far in advance it isn't even worth trying. And yet you call up only a few minutes before you want to eat and you get a table?"

"Of course," Alec replied. "This way."

He walked to a private elevator which opened immediately for him. He waited for Helen to enter but held back his chuckle at her obvious irritation as she followed at a slower pace, every movement of her slender figure showing him her irritation.

They rode down the elevator in silence and stepped out into a parking garage where his chauffer was already waiting with the back door open. Two other men stepped into an SUV parked behind the limousine while a third stepped into the passenger seat next to the chauffer.

"Who are they?" she asked, slightly nervous of the angry looking men with black suits and suspicious bulges at their sides.

"My security detail," he replied curtly before putting a hand to her back and urging her into the car.

Helen watched nervously until they were all in the vehicle. As soon as the door closed, the car sped away.

She sat in the back of the limousine, her arms crossed over her chest and wondered when she had agreed to have dinner with him. This was crazy! She should demand that he pull the vehicle to the curb and let her out.

Just as her head turned towards him and her mouth opened up, he stopped her with a simple denial. "No," he said, obviously reading her mind.

Helen decided to play dumb, give herself time to formulate a response. "No, what?" she asked, knowing he couldn't really be reading her mind.

"No, I'm not letting you out of the car. So sit back and enjoy the ride. We'll be at the restaurant in a moment."

Helen tried not to show her increased irritation at the accuracy of his mind reading but she couldn't stop the small huff of irritation. "How did you...?" she started to say.

Alec laughed, enjoying the expressions flitting across her face. She was beautiful yes, but still young and everything she was thinking was transparent on her face. "Your eyes darted to the door handle and then scanned the sidewalk, Helen. I didn't have to read your mind. Reading your body language and facial expressions is easy enough."

He chuckled at her disgruntled expression, then let his eyes go lower. Did she realize that her arms were pushing her breasts higher? That he could see her nipples through the thin layer of her shirt? Did she have any idea how desirable she looked right at the moment?

"What do you do, Mr. Dionysius?" she asked, desperately wanting some way to get him to stop looking at her. She was embarrassed that he could read her so easily and wanted to figure him out as well. Any clue she could garner from conversations that might give her the upper hand, if only for a moment, would make her feel much better, more in control.

"Call me Alec, Helen. And what do you think I do?"

Helen shrugged her shoulders. "I can't imagine. I'm guessing you're pretty awful."

His eyebrows went up at her reply, both in amusement and surprise at her audacity. "Why would you say that?"

She smiled impishly, loving the fact that she was about to give him a good set-down. "Obviously a lot of people hate you. Otherwise, you wouldn't need the extra body guards. I'm guessing they're here to keep the angry hoards at bay?"

Alec laughed softly. "Yes, at times, they keep the paparazzi out of the way. But they have other purposes."

"What would those other purposes be?" she asked, wishing she knew who he was. She felt at a disadvantage. He looked like he knew so much, whereas, she barely knew his name.

"I don't think you want to know," he said simply and enjoyed the frustration in her beautiful green eyes. He wasn't just being annoying. He didn't want to worry her about the potential threats that he received occasionally or the fact that, due to his wealth, there was a constant danger of kidnapping. They might live in the civilized world where these things were more rare. But they weren't unheard of and unscrupulous people would do a lot for even a fraction of the money in only one of his bank accounts.

Helen eyed him carefully before shrugging and looked down. "I probably don't although not telling me details leaves much to the imagination." She laughed and peeked back at him before saying, "I can imagine a lot of things people might want to do with you."

Alec threw back his head and laughed before his amused glance settled back on her delicate features. "Yes, and I can imagine several things I would like to do with you," he countered and was rewarded by seeing her soft skin turn pink once again.

She should never have dared to challenge him, she thought to herself. He could dish it out much better than she could. "More evidence that you need those guards," she grumbled. "You never mentioned what you do, Alec. I'm guessing you're in investments or something boring like that."

"Why are investments boring?" he asked, neither confirming nor denying her question.

Helen shrugged. "I don't know. It just seems like a horrible life to be stuck in an office all day, never really getting outside and seeing what's going on?"

"I guess you get to do a lot of that in your line of work?"

She smiled and nodded eagerly, unconsciously shifting her body as her excitement increased. "Oh, yes. I love watching people and making up stories about them. Sitting in the park or at a coffee shop, I get to see so many people, all of them rushing around, working or just reading something as they relax. Sometimes I catch interesting people through my camera and I can't wait to get back to my flat and develop the pictures to see if I captured their expressions in the same way I saw them on the street."

"You make up stories about them?" he asked, stunned at the possibility.

"Of course." She looked at him with a curious expression. "Don't you?"

"Never." It would never occur to him to create a fantasy world around people he'd never met and wouldn't ever meet. He preferred reality to make-believe. But the fact that this fascinating woman did this, it created a whole new layer of appeal for him. "What kinds of stories to you make up about the various people you see?"

Helen looked out the window of the limousine, a dreamy smile on her face as she thought about some of the people she'd seen today. "Oh, I don't know. Lots of things. If there's a couple, I look at their body language. If they're stiff and smiling politely, I assume they're on their first date and wonder about the conversations they're having, what new information they're discovering about their potential life mate. If they're angry, then they're having a fight about which school their kids should attend or maybe about the color of the sofa they want to purchase..." she stopped and looked back at his face, noting the ever present amusement. "Don't you ever wonder what other people are thinking?" she asked, more curious now than angry.

"No."

Helen scowled back at him. "Of course you don't," she said, obviously miffed. Tilting her head, she looked at him carefully. "You don't like people very much, do you?"

Alec hesitated with his answer, not wanting to disillusion her or the pretty way she viewed others. "Let's just say that I get to see a different variety of people in my day to day life that doesn't lean towards possible romantic outcomes."

Helen surveyed him, saw the cynicism in his eyes and felt sad for him. Odd, she thought as she looked at his dark, mysterious eyes, ten minutes ago she wouldn't have guessed that she'd actually feel sorry for a man as obviously strong and wealthy as Alec. "I guess you see the bad in people a lot."

Alec didn't answer, but simply shrugged.

"And that's why you have the security detail?"

Alec was suddenly uncomfortable with the perceptiveness of her comments and the way she was looking at him, as if she could see some sort of hurt inside him that simply didn't exist. He didn't really answer her question but said instead, "I protect my privacy."

Helen grinned. "You mentioned the paparazzi. Are they really that bad? Are you some sort of movie star?"

Alec laughed. "I guess you don't get to the movies very often, do you?"

She grimaced. "Not really. People on the street or in a playground are much more interesting than a group of actors spewing out the lines someone else wrote for them to speak. Life is more interesting as it happens." Then she realized she might have insulted him and looked worried. "You're not really an actor, are you?" she asked, pained to think she might have hurt his feelings.

Alec couldn't believe what a soft heart she had. He was shocked to watch the mischievous look turn to true concern over the possibility of him being upset at her words. "No, I'm not an actor."

She instantly relaxed. "Whew!" she gushed and leaned back against the soft leather seat. "I was worried for a moment."

"We're here," he said and couldn't believe he was actually disappointed. The truth was, he wanted to stay and talk to her in private. She was fascinating and he was concerned that she would change once they were in a more public setting. Having no alternative, he stepped out of the car, then turned to offer his hand to help her out.

Out on the street in front of the restaurant, Helen looked at the other elegantly dressed people entering the building and stopped.

He'd stepped away from the curb, intent on walking into the restaurant when he realized she was frozen to her spot on the sidewalk.

"What's wrong?" he asked, coming to stand in front of her so he could see her face, his height blocking out the street lights so they were mostly in shadow.

Helen looked up at him, the worry coming through in her eyes. "I can't go in there dressed like this," she said, holding out her dark green skirt which had seemed fine for running around London taking pictures but was completely inappropriate for an elegant dinner at one of the most exclusive restaurants in the city.

He looked down at her clothes and shrugged his shoulders. "I like it," he replied.

Helen shook her head in exasperation. "Alec, just because you like it doesn't mean it's appropriate. You can't just make everyone else accept a different dress code. I'll be kicked out of the restaurant and even you can't make them accept casual dining attire."

He moved closer, towering over her with his height and broad shoulders. "Back at my office, you argued it would be impossible to obtain a table." He gestured to the famous restaurant behind him. "And here we are." His eyes moved to watch her lips as her teeth nibbled at the lower one. "When are you going to accept that I can, and will, do what I want and obstacles are really not an issue?"

Helen grimaced, conceding his point, wanting to step back to gain a little more space, but she'd fall off the curb if she did so. "Okay, so you have a lot of clout," she grumped, pressing her hands against his broad chest. Unfortunately, he didn't move and she had to look up at him, her stomach muscles clenching with unfamiliar feelings that she wasn't sure she liked. "But that doesn't mean I'll be comfortable dressed in this outfit while dining in a restaurant like The Westin." She waved her hand to indicate people walking along the sidewalk. "Look around you Alec. These people are wearing clothes that cost more than I earn in several months. I don't belong here."

He moved imperceptivity closer, his eyes holding hers intently. "As I see it, you have three options."

"Only three?" she teased, trying to make him smile which might make him a little less intimidating and overwhelming.

He didn't smile, nor did he move back to give her space. His eyes glittered with his intent which only made Helen more nervous when she saw it. "Only three. You can go in there dressed exactly as you are, ignore the other patrons and enjoy the evening with me."

She didn't like that one very much. "And option number two?"

"We can walk across the street and I will buy you that very lovely red dress hanging in the window of the boutique," he said.

Helen looked across the street and her mouth dropped open. The store was Dior and the dress was incredibly lovely but possibly cost over ten thousand dollars. The store was also closed for the night and she didn't relish the idea of Alec bringing the salespeople back to work at this time of the night, regardless of the commission they'll most likely bring in for the sale.

Looking back at him, she shivered. "And option number three?"

Instantly Helen knew this would be the least palatable. The look in his eyes was too pleased and sensuous for her to accept this one. "We go back to my place and my chef cooks us dinner. That would be my preference of the three possibilities since I'll have you all to myself and we can dispense with the formalities of a first date and I can simply take you to bed where we both would enjoy."

Helen glared at him and hid her shaking hands behind her back. "You're kind of a caveman, aren't you? Just hit the woman over the head and drag her off somewhere."

He smiled slowly and she gasped as his hand snaked around her waist, pulling her the last inch so she was flush against him. Her hands automatically came to his shoulders to steady herself and she had a hard time not moving them up around his neck. Instead, she fisted them against his arms, swearing to herself that she wasn't tempted to reach up and touch him, find out what his skin felt like and if the heat radiating inside her was due to his temperature, or something else altogether.

"You like my caveman tactics," he countered, his head dipping lower.

"Says who?" she argued, her chin going up a notch to contradict his statement.

"Says your body." His hand reached up and touched the pulse at her throat which only increased it to a dangerous level. Helen's breathing increased and she had a hard time catching her breath. "You can lie to me with those beautiful lips all you want but your body tells me the truth."

"No. Not...." She started to say, terrified and confused by what he was making her feel.

He stopped her with his finger against her mouth, his head shaking back and forth. "No lies between us."

She hesitated for a long, tense moment. Then finally, she closed her mouth and tried to relax, not saying a word. Her conscience wouldn't let her lie once again but a promise to her Papa a long time ago wouldn't let her tell the truth either. And the truth was frightening. She wanted this man to do things to her that were forbidden until she was married. She'd promised her Papa that so many years ago, given her word that she wouldn't have sex before marriage. He'd been so adamant that she not be "one of those women" as he'd constantly referred to them and he'd made her swear that she'd never blacken the family name by doing something so disastrous. And here she was, in front of a famous restaurant being held in the arms of a man that made her wish she'd never promised her father anything.

Growing up, her father had constantly explained that there were two kinds of women, those that a man married, cherished and respected, and there were those that he had fun with but never showed respect, and never married but instead ridiculed behind her back to his friends. He'd begged her to become the kind of woman a man married and not shame the family name. She'd agreed easily, wanting her father to be proud of her and not ashamed. Family was everything to her and she didn't have the heart to do anything that would bring shame to him or her family.

At the time, she'd only been out dating men for a couple of years and so far, hadn't been very impressed. Ever since then, she'd kept her dates casual, enjoying the company of men, but never going so far as to become intimate with any of them. Never had she even been tempted.

She hadn't met Alec then. He was unlike any of the men she'd met or dated. He was definitely in a class all his own.

After a long, pregnant moment, he released her and Helen breathed a sigh of relief as she worked quickly to get her thoughts and body under control. It was difficult because, although he'd released her, he was still close. She could still smell his cologne and his male scent and she wanted to move closer, to run her fingers through his hair, to have his lips touch hers and feel his strong hands against her body once again.

Turning slightly to the side, she took a deep breath.

"So which option are you going with?"

She bit her lower lip, concentrating. "Let me get this straight. I can either go inside as is, let you spend thousands of dollars on a dress, or go home with you. Does that summarize the options adequately?"

He didn't hesitate. "Yes."

She crossed her arms over her stomach and shook her head. "What about option number four? I just leave here and go home alone, never to see you again."

He stepped closer and shook his head, one finger moving to her cheek, touching her skin and sending fire along her nerves. "That wouldn't be a good choice, my beauty. Helen was instantly immobilized by his touch, barely able to breathe or move. And she dared not move her head so that he was touching more of her. That would be wrong. Suicide, even. "If you went with that choice, we wouldn't get to explore this attraction we both feel for each other," he said and covered her protest with his finger before she could utter the first word to contradict

16

him, "and I would fire Mick and Edna by morning."

Her eyes widened with horror. "You wouldn't do that!"

His expression told her instantly that he would. This man did not bluff. "I would call the head of my human resources and have them instantly terminated for letting you into my office. But you're not going to take that choice, are you Helen? And not simply because I would fire them. You're curious about me. You want to go into that restaurant and find out something about me, anything that would get your mind off of this attraction that has fired up between us. Something that will negate what you're feeling."

"I don't need to do that."

"You do," he contradicted softly. "Because if you don't, you'll go home tonight and wonder, try to work out this puzzle we've created between us but your mind won't have enough facts. You'll still be trying to work things out." He paused for a long moment, letting his words sink in so she could realize the truth in what he'd said. "And for one other reason."

"What's that?" she whispered, trying desperately hard to fight the attraction, the hypnotic spell he was weaving but she couldn't deny the truth of what he was saying either. She fought it, but her heart, as well as her mind, knew that he was absolutely right on target.

"You also want to find out that I'm not as good as you think I am. You want to find a weakness in me, something that will make you dislike me and discount the attraction we're feeling, the attraction your determined to fight for some strange reason."

She stared at him, her mind sifting through his words and knowing that he was right on target with what she was feeling. Helen shook her head, defeated. "As is, then."

His only response was a slight raising of a dark eyebrow before he accepted her decision. He turned and walked away, heading into the restaurant.

Helen looked up at him for a moment, her eyes mutinous. She started to take a step, but then stopped herself, crossing her arms over her chest. She waited until he realized she wasn't next to him. He slowly walked back to where she was standing.

"Is something wrong?" he asked with no expression on his face.

"Even cavemen had manners occasionally," she quipped.

His eyes showed his amusement. "Am I to understand that you're not satisfied with my manners?" he asked.

She shrugged slightly. "A little charm wouldn't go amiss," she pointed out.

It took a moment, but then he threw back his head and laughed.

It took him a long time to get his mirth under control but eventually, he looked down at her, a smile still on his face as he said, "I will endeavor to be more charming. Will that get you into that restaurant? I've been up since four o'clock your time this morning, and have gone through six time zones and can honestly say that I'm not really sure what time I last ate. I'm starving."

Helen rolled her eyes, although she couldn't completely suppress her amusement. "You're horrible," she said but took the arm he offered her, slipping her hand onto his elbow and allowed him to lead her into the elegant, exclusive restaurant filled with all the movers and shakers of the business world, and beyond. If you wanted people to know you'd 'made it' The Weston was the place to be seen.

The maitre'd didn't even blink at her casual clothing. Instead, he and the rest of the wait staff practically gushed over the honor of serving Alec Dionysius and his guest. Helen looked at him curiously as they were led through the dining room. When he dismissed the waiter who held out Helen's chair, preferring that he do it himself, Helen suspected that she might be in trouble.

He seated her, but as he walked around the table, his hand brushed her neck and shoulder, sending shivers of awareness throughout her whole body. She inhaled sharply and looked up at him as he sat down. She gritted her teeth against the sexual tension caused by his casual touch when she caught the triumphant look in his eye. He knew exactly what he was doing and was simply toying with her. Did he have any idea how inexperienced she was? Was she just an easy target for him? Damn the man! That wasn't fair!

She leaned back in her chair and watched him select a wine with the wine steward. He was extremely knowledgeable and she was stunned when he chose a bottle of red wine, one of her favorites whenever she visited her father in Greece. She couldn't afford it here in London but that was her choice. She could live with her father all year round, but that would hurt her mother's feelings. The two had been separated for more than twenty years but never divorced. Her mother, Elisia Miller had met her father more than thirty years ago. They'd met and married within one month, having fallen in love at first sight. Unfortunately, the two were complete opposites. Elisia was a free spirit, loving life and willing to flit from job to job just so she could experience more of whatever struck her fancy. She was a wonderful mother who had taught Helen that life was breathtaking, showed her all the exciting things that nature could provide and what one could do if she followed her dreams.

Helen's father, on the other hand, was a powerful Greek shipping tycoon who had a very strict way of living his life. Her father was in the office each morning at six thirty and didn't leave until seven or eight o'clock at night. When he arrived home, he expected his wife to be there, smiling with a martini in her hand, ready to hear about his day and commiserate with all of the trials and tribulations he'd experienced while at the office. He was strictly regimented and had grown his empire well since he'd taken over from his father.

But Helen's father expected the kind of marriage his parents had, both of whom were still living and had never approved of Elisia nor her marriage to their only son, although they doted on Helen horribly. Being the only granddaughter had its advantages.

Helen had grown up spending the school year in London with her English mother and her summers in Greece with her very Greek father. In London, she'd investigated so many neighborhoods, having lived in a different one every year of her life. Other children might become nervous of that kind of lifestyle, never feeling secure about where one would be living next. But Helen loved it. It might be because she always had her ultra steady father to ground her with solid morals and a large home she could always come back to during her summers.

It could also be because she'd learned how to genuinely appreciate life through her mother, never taking anything very seriously, and then learned to dig in and find a career that she loved and could thrive in with her father. Being a freelance photographer gave her the best of both worlds. She definitely had a career path and the ambition to sell her photos to the more prestigious magazines, even one day to publish her own book. But it also gave her the freedom to come and go as she pleased, to float from one area of the world to the next and appreciate, really look and understand, what was around her.

As she stared across the table at Alec while he finished ordering the wine, she wondered what kind of upbringing he'd had. She guessed it was more along the lines of her father. With a name like Dionysius, he had to be Greek. But how "Greek" was he really? Did he believe in family the way her father did? Did he believe that connections and community were as sacred and inviolate as she considered? Helen doubted it. Many people could trace their ancestry to Greece, could even claim they believed in family above all things, but when it came down to it, they were much more Western than they wanted to think. And would Alec agree with her need for chastity until she married? She hadn't met a man yet who understood, hence the reason she had so many male friends, and no boyfriend. Not wanting casual intimacy was a difficult conversation to undergo in a relationship. Men usually couldn't handle it.

And to date, no man had even tempted her to challenge that.

Not that Alec was tempting her, she told herself firmly.

Goodness, that was a lie!

She sighed and adjusted the napkin nervously. She had to get out of this dinner unscathed but she wasn't sure how she was going to do that. Looking up, her breath froze in her chest. The look he was giving her was lethal and she wanted to look away but couldn't.

"Tell me about yourself, Helen."

She played with the edges of the linen napkin, curling them about her fingers, re-aligning the perfectly straight flat ware, taking a sip of her water, anything that would let her avoid looking into his eyes. "What do you want to know?"

"How did you get into photography, first of all?"

She sighed. This was a safe subject at least. Leaning her elbows on the table, she looked at him now. "That's easy. I love looking around and seeing things. When I realized I could capture whatever I was looking at permanently on film or digitally, I couldn't put a camera down."

"Where did you study photography?"

She laughed softly. "Actually, I went to Harvard in the United States and studied business. I only studied photography by sneaking into the community college during the weekends of each school year. My father wouldn't let me study something so 'flighty' as photography or anything arty is how he phrased it. So I studied business, genuinely enjoyed my classes, earned my degree and now I take the most fascinating pictures I can." She smiled at the end of her tale as if that explained everything.

"You didn't like business?" he asked, not accepting that as the end of the story.

"Oh, no. I love business. I find economics and math very interesting. The theory behind many of the economic models is fascinating and I use that philosophy to take better pictures. Applying economics to peoples' motives gives every individual depth and dimension. You can't take money out of the world. It just won't work. Why fight it?"

"So why didn't you get a job with some company where you could utilize your business skills?"

Helen laughed, having had this conversation with her father over and over again throughout the years. He simply couldn't understand her need to be creative instead of numbers oriented. "It isn't me," she said with a slight lift of one shoulder. "What about you?"

"I went to Oxford, got out and now I use my business degree," he said easily.

She laughed merrily at his synopsis. "And what do you do for fun? What relaxes you?"

"Sex," he said simply, leaning forward and looking into her eyes, daring her to reply to his challenge.

Helen couldn't help the laughter that bubbled up at his response. She looked him up and down and shook her head. "I don't believe you're that much of a roué. You're too intelligent to have sex as your only out-let."

He leaned his elbows on the table, mirroring her posture. "Oh? And what else do you think relaxes me?"

She studied him for a moment. "I think you work out physically like a maniac."

He shifted in a way that told Helen that she was right on target, and that he didn't like that she saw through him. "And what makes you think that?"

She raised an eyebrow, a perfect imitation of his look of interest. "I felt your muscles when we were outside on the sidewalk. Don't even try and tell me you don't enjoy exercise. Those muscles are too hard for someone who only works out for their health."

"Perhaps it's a way to help me concentrate."

"Isn't that the basis for all enjoyment and relaxation?"

"No."

She couldn't help but laugh at his serious expression. "You're wrong," she said, shaking her head.

He raised his eyebrows but moved on to the next subject. They discussed everything and Helen was astonished at how charming the man could be when he put his mind to it. It was as if she'd challenged him and now he was out to prove her wrong.

The meal was extraordinarily delicious as well and over far too quickly, although she glanced at her watch and realized they'd been there for almost three hours, talking and eating and she honestly could say that she couldn't remember laughing so much in a single evening.

When she realized it was almost midnight, she glanced up shyly. "I need to get home," she admitted. "But it's been a wonderful night. I hate to say it, but I really appreciate you coercing me into this meal."

Alec leaned back in his chair, sipping his brandy slowly as he contemplated a strategy for getting her back to his penthouse and into his bed. His body simply would not accept that she wasn't coming home with him. He'd been aching since he'd held her in his arms out on the street. The need to possess her, to somehow put his stamp of possession on her and claim her as his and his alone, was raw and urgent. He didn't investigate these new feelings accepting that there were just some things in life he could take on intuition. As soon as he had her, made love to her and found out her secrets, she would be out of his blood.

"You haven't finished your coffee," he pointed out. "And I don't think I want to let you leave yet."

Helen laughed. "I'm not sure that's possible. I have a meeting tomorrow morning and, although it isn't early, I need my beauty sleep." She pushed her napkin onto the table beside her plate, preparing to stand up.

"Stay with me tonight," he said softly. "I'll make sure you get to your meeting tomorrow with plenty of time to spare."

He watched the momentary indecision in her eyes, felt her gaze drift down over his shoulders and chest. But then her eyes hardened and she stiffened, as if it took a great deal of effort to turn him down.

Helen couldn't deny she was tempted but she had a promise to live up to. "I can't. I won't even explain because you wouldn't understand but I made a promise to someone and I can't break that promise."

Alec stiffened with anger. "Was this promise made to another man?" he asked, his tone just as soft but with a deadly force which was undeniable. Alec couldn't even consider that she might be attached, even casually, to another man. The feelings that were shooting through his system were new and unrecognizable, but as a man, he reacted to them at a primal level. He would not allow any other man to touch Helen, not while he was still interested in her, he told himself.

Helen looked at him curiously. She could sense his anger but didn't understand it. What had she done or said to make him so furious? "Yes. Of course, but I don't see what..."

His brandy plunked down on the table with a thunk and he leaned forward, his dark, dangerous eyes capturing her green ones and holding her captive. "Let's get something straight, Helen. From now on, you make promises to no one but me. Is that clear?" His voice was firm and he thought she would understand that he was not going to stand for her being with another man, no matter what the circumstances.

Helen was stunned for a long moment, blinded to his logic by the intensity of his tone and his gaze. But slowly, she realized that he was ordering her about, thinking he had the right. And stubborn woman that she was, she'd always fought against any kind of authority, driving her father crazy until he'd figured out how to deal with his stubborn daughter.

She shook her head, instantly irritated. "Alec, I'm not sure what you're expecting here but I'm not making promises to you at all. And this promise was made long before I ever met you and I'm not going back on my word." She stood up and pushed her chair in, ignoring the waiter hovering nearby and Alec's security detail that was instantly alert. "Thank you for a very pleasant evening and please, don't do anything about Mick's or Edna's transgression. It was my fault."

Alec was livid that she would walk away after making that kind of a statement. Didn't she know who he was? What he could do to her and her family? With only a phone call, he could destroy her career, ensure that she never sold another photograph. "Sit down, Helen. We haven't finished with this discussion," he articulated carefully.

Helen couldn't believe this man. Where had all the charm gone? Where was the man who had made her laugh throughout the meal and who had listened to all her dreams as if he really cared about her goals and ambitions? He was definitely not this stern autocrat who thought she would jump at whatever commands he wanted to deliver.

She pulled out her wallet, grimacing at the small number of bills left after her lunch. "I'm sorry, I know this won't cover my half of the meal, but it's all I have. Goodnight, Alec," she said and walked away from the table. A part of her wished he would stop her, to take the decision out of her hands. She suspected that, once he started kissing her, she would fall easily into his bed.

Alec watched her as she walked gracefully through the tables, his body rebelling at his patience. He'd have her, he knew. It was just a matter of time. He knew he could convince her but that wouldn't be as good as if she came to him willingly.

"Follow her," he said to Dominic, one of his bodyguards. The man nodded immediately and turned to leave the restaurant.

He then looked down at the table and burst out laughing. The impertinent woman had left him nine pounds. He chuckled as he stood up, shaking his head in exasperation. He'd have to eliminate that stubborn and independent streak she had, he thought. The meal had cost more like nine hundred dollars but he admired the fact that she'd emptied her wallet for him. She obviously had no concept of how much a meal in this kind of establishment could cost but he didn't mind. At least she wasn't after him for his money.

He ducked into the back of his waiting limousine, his mind automatically starting to focus on what he would do once he finally had her in his bed. The ideas flashed through his mind and he shifted uncomfortably as his body reacted to his mind's plans for the slender beauty.

When she reached the sidewalk, Helen quickly raised her hand to hail a cab. She should probably take the bus but she had no idea where the nearest bus stop was or what time it would arrive at this time of night. It was safer, if much more expensive, to take a cab tonight, even though she'd have to charge it to her credit card, something she hated doing since she never knew where, or how much, she'd earn in a month.

Glancing back at the restaurant, she wished the nice part of the evening could have gone on longer. Alec definitely was a different kind of man than what she was used to. She'd never met anyone quite like him. If only he hadn't changed so drastically at the end of the night....

No, she thought as the cab turned a corner and the restaurant's lights faded, Alec was dangerous. His touch could make her forget. She needed to stay away from him completely. He definitely wasn't the man for her.

Chapter 2

Helen balanced the chocolate cake in one hand while talking on her cell phone with the other. "Are you sure you're free for at least an hour?" she asked Edna as she walked quickly around the corner. The building was in sight but she hesitated, hoping she wouldn't run into Alec again. Once had been bad enough. The man had infiltrated her dreams every night for the past seven days and she'd become distracted at least several times a day while working. What had the man done to her? She couldn't get him out of her mind! Men never got under her skin like this. And she definitely didn't like that!

Edna smiled through the phone. "Yes, he's flying back from an international meeting today so I expect him at some point. But thankfully he won't be back until tonight."

"Which is why you're working late, huh?" she asked, feeling hopeful that her plans would all work out. Edna had no idea what was going on, and Helen hoped to keep it that way, at least for a few more minutes.

Edna sighed. "Yes. But things always turn out for the best," she replied.

Helen wasn't fooled. She heard the sadness in her new friend's voice and was determined to make her feel better.

"Okay, then I'll call Mick and let him know I'm on my way. I have a great surprise for you." She hung up the phone quickly, afraid she'd reveal too much if she didn't get off the line immediately.

She saw the woman across the street that looked exactly like a younger version of Edna and waved her free hand. When they were all in front of the enormous steel and glass building, she smiled and stuck out her hand. "Are you Nancy?" she asked eagerly.

"Yes. And this is Jonathan," she replied, shaking Helen's hand

25

while indicating her small son who was standing beside her, an excited look on his face.

The little boy's chubby face broke out into a grin, his excitement almost palpable. "Is Gramma really going to be there? Will she be free? She's never free," he said, a look of uncertainty crossing over his adorable, freckled features.

Helen laughed, enjoying the little boy's enthusiasm. "I just got off the phone with her and she's only expecting me. I told her to expect a surprise but I don't think she knows you'll be there too. You're going to make her day!" Helen fluffed his hair and he looked up at his mother happily.

Helen was charmed. Bending down to his level, she smiled brightly and nodded down at his neat and tidy attire. "I can tell that you went through a great deal of effort to make today special for her," Helen said, indicating his freshly pressed shirt and tie.

"She's my Gramma!" he said as if that were the most important job in the whole world. "I have to look nice for her birthday," he explained with absolute seriousness. And according to this little man, the job of being a grandmother was probably the most important role to fill. Helen admired children for their black and white view of the world. Their perceptions were so pure and simple, it made being an adult look un-necessarily complex.

"Do you think she'll like chocolate cake?" Helen asked, bending down, only vaguely aware of her own mother coming to a breathless stop beside her. All her attention remained focused on the little man puffing up with pride that he might know something special about the woman they were going to visit.

"It's her favorite!" he exclaimed. Then he grinned widely. "And I like it too."

The three women laughed.

Helen scrunched up her nose, looking at the boy conspiratorially. "Okay, well, let's go inside and talk to Mick and see if he'll let us sneak by him one more time. Are you ready?"

She took a moment to greet and hug her mother, introducing Nancy to her mother and vice versa. They all gave a conspiratorial smile to each other when Helen explained that Edna's boss was out of the country for at least a few more hours.

The five of them nodded and they marched inside. Along the way, Helen turned to Elisia, her mother, and smiled her thanks for joining them. "You're going to love Edna."

Elisia grinned right back at her daughter, giving her a small hug. "I'm sure I will. And from everything you've told me about her and her horrible boss, I'm glad I was able to be here today. She sounds like she really needs a break."

Helen stifled her defense of Alec, but just barely. She could just imagine her mother's curiosity if Helen had countered the "horrible" adjective. Had Helen really painted him as that bad in her conversations with her mother? She'd described how Edna worked long hours and was afraid to ask for the day off for her birthday, but Helen also knew that she wasn't very objective when it came to discussing Alec. She'd been careful to leave off a description of the handsome man, but possibly some of her anger over his last order came through in her discussions with her mom.

Inside the building, Mick immediately smiled as Helen approached. "What trouble are you going to cause today, Ms. Helen?" he asked and leaned forward to smile down at Jonathan.

The little boy knew his cue. "Today's my Gramma's birthday!" he exclaimed.

Mick chuckled at his eager explanation for his presence. "And who's your Gramma?"

Helen grinned. "Edna's up in the tower and can't get off today. We brought her chocolate cake and a 'Happy 21st Birthday' candle. Think you could look the other way?"

Mick looked warily at the small cluster of people. "Where's the boss man today?"

Helen's smile instantly disappeared, worry and concern replacing her excitement. "You didn't get into any trouble last time, did you?" She'd definitely have a word with that arrogant man if he'd said anything to Mick.

Mick waved his hand and shuffled his feet slightly. "Nah, he hasn't said a word," Mick replied. "I'm not sure what you said to him but thank you."

Helen was glad no repercussions had fallen on either Mick or Edna for her little adventure last week. She suppressed the disappointment she felt at the lost opportunity to confront him. She denied that she had been looking forward to an excuse to see him again. That was ridiculous she argued with herself for a moment. The man was demented with his own power and arrogance, thinking he could just order someone around and they would simply fall into those orders. Good grief!

Mick laughed and shook his head. "Don't worry about it this time. Edna already called down to set you up with a visitor's badge." He looked behind Helen to the others. "She didn't mention there would be others. "What's going on?" he asked.

Helen smiled brightly. "Today is Edna's sixty-sixth birthday. We have a chocolate cake for her." She turned to the others in the group. "This is Nancy, Edna's daughter and her son, Jonathan. And my mother. We're all going to surprise her with a birthday cake."

Mick laughed, delighted as he handed all of them visitor's badges. "Hold on. Let me get Joe to cover the front desk and I'll come on up with you. Edna's a good woman and she didn't look too happy this morning." He immediately picked up the phone and dialed a number, arranging for his friend to cover the front desk for the next fifteen minutes. Joe arrived quickly and Mick picked up his walkie talkie and waved the group to the elevators.

In the elevator, four more people heard what was going on and all wanted to help with the surprise, each of them had experienced help from Edna's generous nature in the past and wanted to celebrate this event with her. As they moved down the executive hallway, the large, boisterous group attracted more attention as others popped their heads out of their offices to find out what all the noise was about. As soon as they heard whose birthday it was, they immediately joined in with the fun.

By the time they arrived at Edna's office, there were twenty people gathered behind Helen as she lit the "21" candle on top of the chocolate cake. They were all standing outside the office, Helen's intent was to surprise Edna at the last moment.

Unfortunately, that plan fell apart because of the number of people wanting to celebrate the kind woman's birthday. The large group couldn't be very quiet so when they actually entered the large reception area where Edna's desk stood, the older woman was staring curiously at the doorway, pen poised over the paper she'd been working on. As soon as she heard the loud, "Happy Birthday" song, she gasped in surprise, her face breaking out with a huge grin. At the sight of her daughter and grandson, she was thrilled, standing up to receive her grandson's enthusiastic hug as he raced into her arms. She was grinning from ear to ear, Jonathan in her arms and tears in her eyes as the song wound its way to the end, Helen holding the cake up to Edna so she could blow out the candle.

The raucous clapping made Edna laugh, shaking her head in excited embarrassment and a fruitless effort to quiet everyone down.

"What did you wish for?" someone from the back called out?

Edna shook her head. "No way. Can't tell. That ruins the birthday wish," she said, hugging her grandson closely for a moment. She was beaming with pleasure and obviously thrilled that everyone had taken time out of their busy schedules to acknowledge her birthday. She looked down at the small cake and then at the large group. "How on earth is everyone going to get a slice of that?"

Helen waved that concern aside. "Don't worry about a thing," she said. "Just grab a bunch of forks from the kitchen and everyone can have a bite. That way, your birthday wish will come true."

The group gladly joined in and within moments, sterling silver forks were obtained from the executive kitchen and passed around to everyone and then the cake made its way through the group with everyone taking a piece, laughing at the concept and the unprecedented event. Almost everyone was saying how they'd never had a birthday cake at work before and Helen was stunned that anyone could survive with so little workday entertainment.

"What the hell is going on here?" a deep voice said from the back of the room.

Helen looked around and groaned inwardly, immediately identifying the owner's voice. Alec. How was it possible that the two times she'd snuck in here, he'd come back early from his meetings? Was fate trying to tease her about this man? Edna swore he was regimented to the point of ridiculous. What kind of luck was Helen bringing upon this company?

She turned and watched as the whole group instantly tensed. One by one, people walked out of Edna's office in silence, their head bowed as if they were trying to hide or ignore the temporary happiness that had come their way during working hours. Some dared to nod at Alec but without the return nod, they too bowed their heads and walked faster.

Edna was horrified, Nancy was quickly trying to round Jonathan up, Elisia was patting Edna's shoulder ineffectually and Helen was simply furious. She had a clear view of Alec while the room cleared out and she glared at him until the employees were all dispersed.

"What are you doing here?" she demanded, hands on hips and facing him full on, obviously ready to do battle.

Alec couldn't believe what he was seeing. A demolished mess of something he suspected was chocolate cake had been placed in his hands moments before everyone had dispersed, his secretary looked as if she were about to keel over with fear, two other women and a child were either staring or glaring at him and the woman for which his security team had been searching for seven days was now facing him as if he were the devil and she was his secretary's savior angel. If he weren't so furious that she'd escaped his team's efforts for the past week, he would laugh at the idea that this tiny little woman was standing up to him despite all the things he could do to her and her family.

As it was, his eyes traveled down her figure, draped in a crazy colored outfit that stopped at her mid-thigh, the loose dress made up of every color in the rainbow in some sort of psychedelic pattern. On someone else, the dress would look ridiculous, overwhelming the wearer. But on Helen, it just looked...right he admitted grudgingly.

Her lustrous hair was barely tamed with a scarf of orange and her ears dangled with something a middle eastern harem woman would be proud of wearing. Her sandals were nothing more than a flat bottom with leather strings tied up across her feet and ankles that traveled up as if they were some sort of boot without the leather top. And his body reacted immediately, which was why he uttered a curse under his breath before walking into the office to dump the remains of the chocolate birthday cake in the trash.

In answer to her question, he wiped his hands disdainfully before turning to glare down at her. "I believe I work here. As do the rest of the people that had been loitering in this office when I arrived. Care to explain?" he growled out to the still furious beauty who had haunted his dreams every night since he'd met her.

Helen wasn't intimidated although she knew that Jonathan was clutching his mother's leg tightly and Edna was about to burst into tears. It wasn't right to be this mean to someone on her birthday and she was just the person to let him know it. "It's Edna's birthday, you insensitive brute!" she said, poking a finger into his stomach. Unfortunately, her finger came away hurt because there wasn't any give to his abdomen. "Why can't you be nice, and just a wee bit sensitive every once in a while? Can't you see that you've ruined Edna's birthday celebration and her grandson is now terrified of you? Or do you simply not care?" She was practically yelling at him when she was finished, so worked up at his attitude that she didn't care what reaction he had to her words.

Helen wished she hadn't touched him and it had nothing to do with the fact that her finger hurt after coming into contact with the steel muscles in his stomach. Anger, she told herself. That was good. Desire? That would be bad. Maintain the anger and get out of here as quickly as possible.

Her mind gave her instructions but her body moved an inch closer. "Aren't you supposed to be somewhere over France right about now?" She smelled him, and wanted to get closer. Not a good reaction, she told herself. Move away. Run, she told her feet. But they stayed put, not moving even an inch as her nose inhaled his masculine scent, noting his spicy aftershave and something that was just....male. And sexy.

Alec leaned toward her, forcing her back an inch. "I was able to get an earlier takeoff. But that's irrelevant," he snapped, unable to believe he'd actually explained himself to her. "What's important here is that you've once again disrupted my staff."

That worked, taking her out of the spell his scent had put her under. Anger returned. She continued to poke him in the chest, emphasizing each word as she spoke, refusing to back down no matter how furious his expression became. "Listen here, buddy. Today is Edna's birthday and you're an awful employer for not giving her the day off to celebrate with her grandson and daughter. And to top it off, you're scaring her grandson," she growled, hearing Jonathan's whimpers behind her. "And that's unacceptable. So make nice and find some small portion of humanity in your heart, if you still have one," she mocked, "and be a gentleman for a small fraction of the day!"

Alec could not believe he was being reprimanded by this tiny woman. Leaders of industry quaked in their shoes when he showed the smallest interest in their company. Rulers of countries called him to ask advice and women threw themselves at him constantly in an effort to gain his attention. And she was yelling at him? Unbelievable!

"In my office," he pointed behind her, glaring down at her face.

Helen didn't move fast enough for him so he took her by the arm. As he passed by Edna who had her head bowed, he snapped out, "Go home Edna. But have the Lindsey contract ready for my review tomorrow morning by nine o'clock," he continued.

At Alec's first words to Edna, Helen had thought he was firing the woman. By the looks on everyone else's face, they'd thought the same thing. So when he continued with instructions for the following day, Helen was too relieved to resist when he pushed her into his office and closed the door.

Then the seriousness of the situation struck her. Edna was leaving, which meant that Nancy, Jonathan and even her mother would be gone from the outer office. She was definitely alone with a man that terrified her, broke down the barricades she'd built to protect her self-control.

Thankfully, her anger reasserted itself and she stomped into the middle of his office, then turned to glare at him. "That was very gracious of you, Alec," she said, her voice dripping with sarcasm. "A few kind words, even a 'Happy Birthday' wouldn't have hurt you. But I guess you're too busy being the head honcho and not letting anyone see that you have a nice part of you, even if it's a small fraction of a cell."

Alec stalked her, taking one step at a time as he said, "I'll have you know that I currently employ over one hundred thousand people in almost every country in the world."

"So?" she bit out, still glaring. "All that proves is that you're merciless."

31

"It also proves, very adequately, that I know how to run a company. One could even go on to say that I'm a very good employer since every employee in this company knows that they will still have a job to come back to in the morning as long as they perform to my standards."

"Perhaps your standards are a bit too high!"

"I beg to differ with you!" he snapped right back at her.

"Beg all you want but the reality is, some of your employees were enjoying a small break and you made a federal case out of it. What does that say about you and your so-called employee relations?" He was almost to her and she wished she could take a step back but she stood her ground, refusing to let him see her retreat. "And I'm not afraid of you. You don't employ me so there's nothing you can do to me."

"You should be," he said softly.

As he closed in on her, she wasn't able to support her anger any longer. Her mind refused to maintain the fury and it was quickly being replaced by his scent, his masculinity, his heat. So she couldn't help it when she lost the thread of the conversation. His mouth was too close and she could smell his spicy aftershave. Her eyes drifted away from his black, scowling eyes and she watched his mouth, her mind running rampant as her curiosity to feel his lips on hers almost overwhelmed her. "Should be what?" she whispered, trying desperately to figure out what was going on.

"Afraid of me. You should be very afraid of me. And understand that there are many things I can do to you. Many things I will do to you. So this is fair warning, Helen."

His meaning slowly penetrated and her entire demeanor changed. Gone was the anger. Unfortunately, it was replaced by the same desire she saw reflected in his eyes. "No," she gasped a moment before she took a step to run away.

That step was halted when his arm snaked out and wrapped around her waist, pulling her up and against him.

Helen was terrified. When his lips covered hers, she couldn't think but pushed against him, her small fists punching against his massive shoulders. But he easily grabbed her arms and held them by her sides, the whole time not relenting on her mouth. It took him less than two seconds before she was no longer fighting him but wrapping her arms around his neck, pressing herself against him and opening her mouth to his, glorying in the feel of his tongue as he invaded her mouth.

Helen whimpered, pulling herself closer, needing to feel him and touch him. She couldn't get enough of him and wasn't sure what she could do to assuage this desperate need that had taken control of her senses.

When she felt his hand on her waist slide up and touch her back, her ribs, she melted even further into the chaos that was rampant in her mind. Something was telling her to run, but the stronger message in her mind was to discover all those mysteries that she'd been thinking about for the last week.

Reaching up, she let her fingers slide into his hair, feeling the softness, her fingers touching his jaw, his hair, his ears and caressing his neck as she found answers to the desperate questions that had been plaguing her nights after their last meal. She didn't want to know, but each time her fingers encountered another texture on this man, her body shivered, reacting and falling just a little deeper under his spell.

"No!" she called out when his hand touched her breast at the same time his teeth nipped at her ear lobe. It was too much and she couldn't understand what was happening to her. The feelings were frightening and she called out a halt, grateful when Alec allowed her the space. Helen pulled back and, in his surprise at her reaction, he allowed her the freedom.

Alec watched in stunned surprise as she backed up, her eyes wide with fear and desire. "Helen?" he asked, taking a step closer but she shook her head, holding her shaking hands up in front of her and closing her eyes. She swallowed and took a deep breath, trying to gather her wits and explain.

"Have you never..."

"No!" she interrupted him and steadied herself against his desk. "No. I haven't. I need to go."

She started to move toward the door but he stopped her by the expedient way of simply stepping in front of her. "I won't let you go. You need to stay and talk to me. If we need to go to a restaurant where others can see us then that's fine."

"Alec," she said, starting to reach up and touch his chest but she pulled her fingers back before she made contact with him. Unfortunately, he was having none of that and took her hand to press it to the middle of his chest. She shuddered and tried to pull her hand away but he wouldn't let her, in fact he moved closer. "I can't," she whispered. "You wouldn't understand. Please just respect the fact that I can't do....this...." she said awkwardly, "with you."

"I won't accept that. And I do respect you. I respect you enough to know that something is holding you back from a relationship with me. I need you to tell me what that is so I can eliminate that obstacle."

Helen had to laugh at his arrogance. He honestly believed there wasn't anything he couldn't fix and make right. Or at least right enough in his mind. "That's very admirable of you but this isn't one of those things that can just go away."

Thankfully, the phone rang at that moment. He sighed and stepped back, releasing her hand. "We're not done with this conversation. We'll finish it as soon as I can get rid of whoever is on the phone."

He turned his back to her and walked around his desk, picking up the phone and snapping out a greeting. Helen listened to him for a moment, trying to decide when would be a good time to escape. He turned around to sort through some documents and Helen knew that this was the perfect time to simply slip out the door.

But she didn't. She stayed right where she was and waited, watching in amazement as he discussed numbers off the top of his head, demanding more information and it was as if she could see the wheels turning inside his mind as he analyzed the data and made decisions. The commands were about monetary values that she couldn't even comprehend, in terms and financial jargon that she'd studied only vaguely in school but had no practical knowledge of. She was simply in awe of his amazing intelligence and it startled her to admit that to herself.

She saw him glance in her direction and it surprised her so much, she almost flinched. What exactly she was waiting for, she wasn't sure. Would Alec listen to the promise she'd given to her very old-fashioned father ten years ago? Would he understand her position and leave her alone? Could they be friends? Looking at his tall body and the muscles rippling underneath the fabric of his shirt, she knew the answer. Alec was not a "friend" kind of man.

She and Alec could never be friends. They could definitely be lovers for as long as the passion lasted but then where would that leave her? Would he marry her? And if he did, how long would that last? Her carefree mother and business oriented father had lasted for only ten years before the inevitable break up. Two completely different souls could not last, especially in this world. Could she and Alec last longer? What would happen to her at the end of their marriage? Would she be able to fall in love with someone else? Her mother hadn't. Deep down, Helen knew that her mother pined for her father almost constantly, that they were both still madly in love with each other and living miserable lives separately.

No, a relationship between herself and Alec made no sense. She had to get away and run as fast as she could from this incredible man. And if she never met anyone like him again? Well, at least she could find someone else before her feelings were too involved. She didn't want to fall in love with Alec and find herself fighting with him all the time, then leaving him because the fights were too much to live with, hurt too deeply or that they found that their love had been killed by the hurt and anger of their fighting.

Taking a deep breath, Helen stood up and walked quietly to the door, slipped out when he was distracted and walked out of the now empty reception area to the elevators. Her heart was beating the entire time, wondering if he would realize she'd left and come after her. A part of her was honest enough to admit she wanted him to do exactly that. She wanted Alec to take the decision out of her hands and make love to her, show her what it was all about and her promise be damned. But she couldn't. That would be breaking her word and she couldn't do that to her father. She loved him and it would break his heart if she became some wealthy man's mistress, which is all she could be with Alec.

Out on the street, she pulled herself together and hurried to the subway station. She had to get out of here. She had a photo shoot tomorrow and she needed to get ready for it. She had things to do and places to go, film to pick up, memory cards for her digital cameras to clear out and download to her computer so they were free for the next day, processing chemicals to purchase. She had to get going and most importantly, never think about Alec, nor come into close proximity with the man that could make her forget a very important promise.

Helen pushed herself until late that night. After she'd gotten ready for the next day, she grabbed her camera and headed out of her tiny apartment. She couldn't stay there and think or she'd go insane so she followed her nose to the park and took pictures of kids on the playground and when it became too dark for children to be out playing, she snapped night shots of the city lights, the cars zooming along the boulevards and the people mingling on the sidewalks, eager to get home to their families or whatever their plans were for the night.

It was after midnight before she allowed herself to crawl into bed. She prayed she would be able to sleep without dreams of Alec invading her mind. He'd been there for the past seven nights. Wouldn't it be nice to have at least one night where she didn't wake up yearning for something that was too dangerous for her to handle?

Chapter 3

Alec was furious! The woman had slipped out of his office and was nowhere to be found. Dammit, how could he not have grabbed her purse and gotten her identification? He didn't even have her phone number. He waited patiently until the following morning when Edna walked in and sat down at her desk.

Strolling out when he heard her start to settle into her routine, he leaned against the edge of her desk. "Did you have a nice afternoon off?" he asked easily enough. He watched in frustration as a look of wariness crept over her face. Was he really that much of an ogre? Was his entire staff afraid of him?

"Yes. It was a nice surprise," she replied stiffly. "Thank you very much and I'm terribly sorry about the party. I had no idea. Helen implied it would only be her," she explained weakly. "But you know Helen," she said with a shrug.

That grated on Alec. He tried hard to not grit his teeth as he answered, "No, actually. I don't know Helen. What about her?" He sat down in the chair in front of her desk and watched her expression soften with affection for the woman who was slowly driving him insane. The fact that anyone could actually accomplish that feat was irritating him to no end. He'd been called cold, emotionless and merciless before by his previous mistresses and business associates. He could just imagine their amusement now if they could see how this one tiny woman had gotten under his skin.

Edna smiled fondly. "Oh, I don't think I know her very well either. I just know she has a personality that people flock to. She can get people to do just about anything. They open up to her because she's just so open and light-hearted herself. People want to be with her, be her friend and she loves humanity too much to ignore anyone that might need her help, even if it's just a simple conversation. Her mother is also delightful. We all had dinner together last night."

That startled him even further, knowing that he'd wanted to have dinner with her himself before she'd snuck out of his office. "Helen was with you?" he asked, trying to keep the jealousy and frustration from his tone.

Edna frowned at his question, her eyes curious as she looked across her desk at her boss who had never had a personal conversation with her in the five years she'd been working for him. "No, actually. Elisia, Helen's mother, couldn't reach Helen. She wasn't answering her phone for some reason so dinner was just with my daughter, my grandson and Helen's mother."

Alec's eyes darkened with concern. "She doesn't answer her mobile? Why have one if you aren't going to answer it?"

Edna was already shaking her head. "Helen has a cell phone, but she only answers it when she remembers to turn it on. Last night was one of those times when Helen wasn't answering for some reason."

Alec could tell that his secretary was concerned about the reasons for Helen's absence and isolation last night but he was in no mood to tell her that he'd lost the impertinent Helen as well after everyone's departure. He focused instead on the idea of Helen wandering around London without any means of communicating in an emergency. "She turns off her cell phone? Is that safe? What would happen if she needed something?"

Edna shook her head. "That's Elisia's worry as well. She's tried to get Helen to turn on her phone more often, but Helen doesn't like the distraction."

Alec's eyebrows drew together in his concern. "Why the hell not? Its every parent's right to protect their child. Helen's just being ridiculous."

"No," Edna denied vehemently, "Helen's not self-centered in any way. She's the most giving person I've ever met. She just very focused on her art and the ringing of her phone would interrupt the process. She's very dedicated to her work. She doesn't accept money from her father either. She lives in a small apartment, refusing her family's money." Edna looked down slightly before saying, "A little like you, Mr. Dionysius."

"Excuse me?" he asked, not sure he'd heard his secretary correctly.

Edna was suddenly uncomfortable. But she continued, "Well, rumors are that your father offered to back you when you started out. You refused and built up all this on your own. It's quite an impressive legacy."

Alec dismissed her insight with a shake of his head, as if another person backing him financially to start his own empire had never occurred to him. "My father has his own business interests."

Edna nodded in agreement. "Helen just wants to make it on her own. She doesn't want people handing it to her."

Alec considered this but still thought that not turning on a phone, especially a woman, especially one as beautiful as Helen, was not right. She could be in all kinds of danger and he felt suddenly uncomfortable, irritable even, at the idea of her walking around the city of London without that kind of security. She was taking an unnecessary risk by not turning on her phone. "How's the Lindsey contract coming along?" he asked, changing the subject.

He thought about asking Edna for Helen's address, then discarded the idea. He suddenly realized that he was enjoying the game of chess with the lovely, irritating woman. Especially after that kiss in his office!

Chapter 4

"Hello?" Helen answered her cell phone absently as she pulled the photos out of the processing chemical. Her bathroom was cramped, but it was the only space where she could process her photos without fear of them being exposed to light before they were ready.

"Helen? Hi, this is Jim. I'm sure you don't remember me but I was the guy standing next to you at Edna's party last week."

Helen pinned the photo up on the string hanging across her shower. "Hi Jim. Of course I remember you. How could I forget a guy wearing such a great tie? All those little bunnies! It was great."

Jim laughed through the phone and Helen could hear him relax. "Yeah, well, that's kind of my little way of lightening things up over there. I usually don't wear things like that when I think Mr. Dionysius is going to be in the office."

She laughed, completely understanding his comment. Alec was mean and tyrannical and she liked the fact that this man was snubbing his nose at Alec's rules and silently getting away with it. "He's kind of a tyrant, isn't he?" Helen said, her nose wrinkling at the idea of anyone being afraid of what they would wear.

"No, no!" he was quick to say. "He's a great boss. I can't believe how much I've learned while working under him. When I first started at Dionysius Corporation, I was one of those fresh out of college know-it-alls. Over the past ten years, I've really learned a great deal and it's all because of Mr. Dionysius' patience and ability to translate his vision to the people who work for him, get us all behind what he's trying to accomplish."

That wasn't what Helen needed to hear right about now. She was pulling out the pictures of the sunset, the ones she'd taken the first night she'd met Alec and she needed to think of him as an awful person.

Someone she could never respect and would never get along with. "Well, I'm sure he's been a hard driving person. You probably work about eighteen hour days, don't you?" she asked, hoping he would give her more reason to not like him.

"Only sometimes," he laughed. "And that's only when I've screwed up and need to fix something. I don't want Mr. Dionysius to know how badly I've messed up sometimes."

Ugh! More bonus points for Alec! "I'm sure he's made many mistakes in the past, Jim. You shouldn't have to put in the extra hours just to keep up with him."

Jim was silent for a long moment. "I think you have the wrong impression of him. He really doesn't work twenty-four-seven. He's a big advocate of work-life balance."

"Hmm..." was all Helen would say. She'd witnessed differently but she wasn't going to argue with him. "So what's up? Why the surprise call?"

Jim chuckled a moment. "Well, I was wondering if you might be interested in a party this Friday night. I've been invited to something spectacular and was hoping you might be free." He was silent for another moment. Then he added, "As a kind of a date. That is..." he started off awkwardly, "I mean...if you don't have any other plans, that is. If you're busy, I completely understand and this would be really bad timing, especially in light of the way you think of Mr. Dionysius. It might not be the best..."

"I'd love to go. What time?" she asked, interrupting any possible defense of the man she was trying very hard to hate. Or even better, just not think about.

She heard his sigh of relief and was charmed by his nervousness at asking her out. "Would it be okay if I picked you up at seven o'clock?" he asked. "The party starts at seven thirty. And it's cocktail dress. I'll be wearing a dark suit," he explained.

"Seven o'clock on Friday night sounds wonderful under one condition."

She heard his gulp. "What's that?"

"You have to wear another one of your great ties."

Jim laughed, obviously relieved that the stipulation was an easy one. "I think I can manage that since it will be after hours. I don't think Mr. Dionysius will mind too much."

Helen had no idea why the man would worry about his employer's tie preferences when the man was out on a date at a party, but she kept her opinions to herself. If he liked working for a man who monitored after hours attire, then he had a lot more to learn about the work place and life in general. And she was just the woman to teach him, she thought.

A project! What a better way to get one man out of her mind? Start dating a new one! Someone who was more along her mental lines – and any man who wore bunnies to work had to have a rebel underneath all that work ethic, she thought. She just needed to bring it out a little more. Helen was always up for a challenge!

"Great. I'll see you on Friday night."

"Fantastic!" he said. "I'm looking forward to it."

When Friday night came around, Helen was actually exhausted. She'd been working long hours just to keep her mind too worn out to think but no matter how much she tried, she ended up dreaming of making love with Alec. She considered calling up Jim and begging off the evening but then remembered how nervous he'd been about calling her in the first place. She could just explain that she had and early shoot in the morning and couldn't stay out late. She could make it up to him by asking him out for a pizza night next week. She would surely be over this silly infatuation with the tall dark and devastatingly handsome Alec by then. She would make sure of it.

Jim arrived at seven o'clock, on the dot. She was just pulling her hair up into a loose knot on her head when he rang so she had several pins in her mouth as she answered the door with one hand while pinning up her mass of curls into a slightly more respectable twist with the other.

She opened the door and stepped back, mumbling, "Come on in Jim. It's good to see you again," she said, extending her hand as a greeting when he walked into her tiny apartment.

Jim looked at her appearance and whistled. "Great dress!" he exclaimed as he tried to find a space in her miniscule family room that wasn't covered with pictures or camera equipment.

She couldn't smile without losing her bobby pins so she winked at him instead. "Thanks. There's a bottle of wine in the fridge. Help yourself while I finish getting ready," she said. Helen walked back into her bedroom, glad she'd chosen the dress now after seeing his reaction. She'd found an antique silk sarong that she'd wrapped low around her waist and matched it with a matching orange silk tank top with sparkles at the neckline. When she'd gotten it home and tried it on, she realized that the silk top was just a little too short, so she'd added a gold belt with small dangling coins to her waist to fill in the gap. So whenever she moved, her gold chain would peek out. She felt pretty and sexy and the admiration in Jim's eyes told her she'd hit the right mood for the night.

Her apartment was tiny with only the family room and galley kitchen in the front with the bedroom and a miniscule bathroom off to the side. Two people couldn't fit into the bathroom at one time and she'd made it even worse since she used it as her dark room. Right now, she had about fifty photos hanging from the ceiling as they dried from the processing chemicals. She watched in the mirror as Jim poured both of them a glass of wine.

He was handsome in a clean cut, nice guy kind of way. He was about four inches taller than she was in her sparkling, gold sandals and he had blond hair and green eyes, looking very sweet. If she'd seen him on the street, she wouldn't have looked at him twice but since he'd been one of the first people to join in the group of singers earlier this week, eager to participate in the impromptu birthday celebration for Edna, she'd been impressed and had smiled at him, remembering him as he sang loudly along with everyone else.

"How do you like the wine?" she asked, fitting the last pin into her hair.

She saw Jim take another surprised sip of the white wine before he said, "It's very good."

She came out of the bedroom and smiled, patting her head once more for luck. "I'm glad you like it," she said, taking the glass he handed her. "It's one of my favorites but recently I found a merlot that I like even better."

He nodded his head and looked around the small apartment. "Did you take all these?" he asked, indicating the pictures on the walls.

Helen smiled with pride. The walls were filled with her photos, some framed, some not. "Yes. I'll splurge on a good bottle of wine but not necessarily frames," she laughed derisively. "Some might say I have my priorities out of whack but that's okay. I'll accept that there might be some truth to that statement and thrive as I open my next bottle of perfect wine."

He walked over to one of the walls and started examining the photos. "They're extremely good," he said after he'd walked by one wall, looking at each carefully. "You have real talent, not just at picking out wines," he winked at her.

"Thanks", she smiled back, truly appreciative of his compliments. He walked around the room, asking questions about the pictures while they drank their wine. Helen was glad to answer all of his questions, not concerned about what they might reveal about herself. She knew that writing was a little more self-expressionistic but photography revealed the inside of the subject if the photographer was good enough, the lighting and angles just right and the subject willing. She could feel the pain or joy of a person when she developed a photo of a person and she could feel that same joy or sorrow when she photographed landscapes.

42

They finished their wine and Jim said they should get going. He was an easy man to talk to and she learned a lot about him in the taxi on the way over to the party. The main thing she learned, unfortunately, was that she was not attracted to him in any way. That thought depressed her initially but she told herself to enjoy the evening with him anyway. He was very nice and intelligent. So what if he didn't stir her senses like some other man who wouldn't be named....or thought of....or considered at all during the next five hours while she was with another man, she told herself firmly.

"Wow!" she said as the taxi turned down the driveway of the house where the party was to be held. "Is this a hotel or something?" she asked, staring at the enormous mansion looming in front of them. It was magnificent. The white brick highlighted the large windows on three stories with ivy growing up two sides. The drive curved around the front entrance which was lined with flowering trees. She had no idea what kind of tree flowered this late in the season but she couldn't believe how beautiful it looked.

Jim laughed softly. "No. Not a hotel. Just a residence. Although not like anything I'll ever be able to afford," he said smoothly. He stepped out of the taxi and paid the driver. Jim came around to the passenger side and offered his arm to Helen who was still staring up at the enormous house. She'd lived with her father during the summers so she understood wealth. Her father lived in a mansion sitting atop a cliff in Athens with extensive gardens and more rooms than the man knew what to do with. But this was on a whole other level than even her father who was considered extremely wealthy by many standards.

A bad feeling seeped into Helen's bones. "Jim, who is hosting this party?" she asked nervously.

"I told you," he laughed softly. "My boss asked all of his upper management to a cocktail party to celebrate the latest acquisition. I was lucky enough to be on the proposal team. This is my second time here but I'm still a little awestruck by the man and his house, to tell you the truth." They were walking up the steps behind several others who were dressed in conservative dark suits for the men and black cocktail dresses for the women. Many were wearing pearls at their throats but a few had diamonds. One or two were wearing white cocktail dresses but Helen's orange and red outfit was by far the most colorful. One might even say outrageous in this company she thought, considering the high necklines and severely tailored dresses on the other women. The most daring accessory she saw was a woman wearing a double strand of pearls, Helen noted, hearing her gold chain tingle as she moved slightly.

"Please tell me you work directly for someone other than Alec

Dionysius, Jim. Please, please tell me that your immediate supervisor is not the owner of your company."

Jim puffed up, a proud smile on his face. "Of course I have managers in between, but I interact with Mr. Dionysius on several issues now that I've been promoted over the years."

She started to pull back and Jim looked at her questioningly. "Is something wrong?" he asked.

Helen swallowed painfully. "I can't go in there," she whispered, dropping his hand and starting to walk backwards. "I'm sorry," she said to him as he paused beside her, the worry already in his eyes. "I just can't do it and you wouldn't want me to be with you anyway. Alec hates me. So I guarantee I'll be a liability to your career."

Jim laughed and grabbed her hand, stopping her and turning her around. His green eyes were amused as he looked at her. "Helen, I don't think Mr. Dionysius even remembers that you were there at Edna's party so don't worry. Besides, with you on my side, I'll be guaranteed to have the prettiest woman in the room. You won't be a liability. You'll be a huge asset. Trust me."

Helen shook her head at the last statement. "You don't understand. He'll definitely remember me from the previous occasions." She didn't go into the details of her kiss with Alec but she could tell that her face was heating up at just the thought of how she'd felt in his arms. Shaking off that memory, she turned to Jim and looked him right in the eyes. "Alec blames me for messing up the smooth operation of his executive staff. It's happened twice recently and each time he's been furious so you don't want to be seen with me."

Jim laughed harder. "Come on. The taxi is already gone and you can't wander around the grounds alone."

"No really," she said, pulling out of his light grasp. "I'll be fine. I'll just wander over to that tree and wait until you're done. It can't be very long. I'm sure Alec will send all of his staff home early enough so they can still get in a few hours of work before you retire for the night."

Jim shook his head, laughing at her suggestion. "You can't wander around the grounds, Helen. There are motion sensors all over the yard. If you accidentally trip one off, a pack of vicious dogs will come out and scare the living daylights out of you." He picked up her hand and tucked it back into the elbow of his arm. "Come along. I promise we'll stay out of my boss's way and I'll introduce you to the others I work with. Unfortunately, I'm not high enough on the food chain to actually know Mr. Dionysius on a very personal level yet so he won't be in our main crush of conversations. He'll be schmoozing with his vice presidents tonight and won't even notice us as we partake of his excellent liquor and possibly the best food you'll ever eat."

Helen was doubtful but she accepted that there would probably be enough people here tonight so she could at least hide in the crowds and be inconspicuous.

Warily, she followed him up the steps once again and into the house. Thankfully, they were late enough that, if there'd been a receiving line, it was gone now and they could enter the house without being greeted by the man himself.

"Come on," Jim said, leading her through the enormous foyer to the back of the house where most of the people were mingling. "You've got to see this place. It's amazing."

Helen had to agree with him. Even having grown up with her father's palace-like house, she was impressed with this one. Jim led her to an enormous living room area that had to be more than five thousand square feet and two stories high. The back wall had Palladian windows on the first level, then another set of enormous square windows on the second story. The room had honey colored hardwood floors that added warmth as well as elegance with large, comfortable looking sofas and chairs placed strategically around the room and large white columns spacing the room geometrically. She counted three groupings of sofas and chairs in this area with a massive fireplace at each end. The hardwood floors were softened in these groupings by large carpets that made the room feel more welcoming.

As she stared out one of the five sets of French doors currently opened onto the patio, she could see more white but this was of stone instead of marble. It extended out to stairs that descended into a formal garden laid out in patchwork with large oak trees framing both sides and marble statuary in the middle. Directly down the center was an Olympic sized swimming pool with floating candles surrounded by flowers dancing on the surface.

"Impressive, isn't it?" Jim mumbled to her as he took two glasses of white wine from a passing waiter. "Mr. Dionysius doesn't scrimp on the entertainment budget, does he?"

"Nor on the home cooling bill," she mumbled, trying desperately to find something about the party she didn't like. She didn't want to be impressed. She didn't want to know anything about the man that might tip the scales in his favor. Already loving his home, she had to find something that was wrong – and the open doors letting the air conditioning out of the house was the best thing she could think of.

Unfortunately, when she mentioned it, Jim only laughed and shook his head. "Don't be too hard on him. I think he uses solar energy for most of the appliances and the air conditioning would be one of them.

It's my understanding that one of his smaller companies is one of those environmental research firms and this house is a sort of test tube for their ideas. This house probably uses less energy than my two thousand square foot condominium."

Drat! Helen hated that little factoid and wanted to find a small corner to hide out in. She sipped her wine and looked around, searching out the one man she'd been avoiding for a week. He must have gotten her phone number from Edna because he'd left her several messages the first few days after their most recent encounter but then she hadn't heard anything. She'd hoped he'd finally given up on her but something told her that wasn't the case. She suspected he was just biding his time. Sort of like a spider waiting for the bug to fly into his web. "I'm sure he's still wasting something," she grumbled.

"I'm sure he does, but then don't we all? However, Mr. Dionysius isn't really in the same league, is he? Men like him live in a whole different world than we do."

Helen looked around at his beautiful home. "Obviously. And these two worlds should stay well apart from each other," she said and took his hand to lead him over to the patio.

Jim was about to grab a plate at the buffet table when one of his co-workers found him. They were engaged in a lively conversation about the acquisition and their excitement that it was finally over. Jim introduced her to several of his co-workers, all of whom were very nice and instantly incorporated her into their conversations as if she were one of them.

Helen had been at the party for perhaps an hour when she finally started to relax. She sipped her wine and smiled at all of Jim's co-workers and their significant others when she started to see Jim's eyes stray to the right several times. Helen followed his eyes in that direction and caught a pretty blond waitress glancing back at him.

When Jim realized that he'd been caught, Helen laughed softly, not taking offense at his distraction since she'd already realized that she wasn't attracted to Jim in that way either. "She's pretty," she said with an encouraging smile.

"Yes, well," he cleared his throat, a blush creeping up his neck and he adjusted his tie slightly. "Let's go say hello to my direct boss. He's over there. Then we can relax and grab something to eat."

Helen looked in the direction he'd indicated quickly to determine which boss Jim was referring to and, when it wasn't Alec, she relaxed. Glancing in the opposite direction she searched for the pretty blond waitress, catching the other woman's eye. Initially the waitress looked away, embarrassed. But Helen already had a mind to do something about this situation. Jim was a very nice man. She wasn't really interested in him as anything more than a friend but the fact that he was being an absolute gentleman and ignoring the blond warmed her heart. She followed Jim and chatted for several more minutes before excusing herself from the group.

She made her way to the bathroom and washed her hands, then searched out the kitchen, determined to find the waitress and find out what was going on. She lucked out and found the woman setting up another tray of creative and delicious smelling appetizers. "Good evening," Helen said, sliding up to the blond and popping one of the appetizers into her mouth. "Oh, these are scrumptious," she said as a way to open the conversation. "Did you help make them?"

The blond looked down, not daring to look into Helen's eyes. "I'm just here doing the serving, ma'am. But I'd be happy to bring you more if you'd like." The waitress said to the tray.

"Jim's a very nice man." Helen said.

The woman stiffened, froze for a long moment before setting the appetizers onto the tray more quickly. "Your boyfriend is an attractive guest."

"Don't worry. He's not my boyfriend. He's just a friend. What's your name?"

That admission perked the woman up for a moment, but then she looked around warily at the other workers, obviously afraid her supervisor would catch her talking to a guest. "I'm Amanda," she said and finished the tray. Picking it up, she smiled at Helen, offering her more food. "Is there anything else I can get you?"

Helen popped another appetizer into her mouth from the counter, not wanting to mess up Amanda's platter. "Just give me your phone number and I'll pass it along to Jim. I know he's interested so I'll tell him to give you a call."

Amanda's eyes widened. "My phone number?" she whispered.

Helen grimaced. "You're right. Work your way around the party and I'll get Jim's phone number so you can call him. It's safer that way. I know Jim and he's very sweet, but a woman can't be too careful." Helen pushed away from the counter and smiled encouragingly at Amanda. "Don't worry about anything. I'll let him know you're a very nice woman and won't be dallied with," she teased.

Amanda instantly laughed and relaxed. "Why would you do this? Why aren't you interested in him?" she asked, dumbfounded that anyone could not find the very nice looking Jim attractive.

Helen took another sip of her wine and sighed. "I don't know. I just know that I'd rather be his friend than anything more. So nothing is going to happen."

Amanda grinned and nodded. "Thank you," she said quickly and with a great deal of sincerity and appreciation.

Helen watched happily as Amanda walked out of the kitchen with a new spring to her step.

Helen followed more slowly, wishing she could feel jealousy at this activity. Shouldn't she feel more possessive of her dates? But then, she'd never felt that way about any of the men she'd dated over the years. She'd even been mildly attracted to some of them but none had ever gone anywhere since she'd ended up friends with almost all of them. Some were happily married now with children and Helen was even invited to the birthday parties and other celebrations.

Sighing in wonder, she walked out of the kitchen and looked around for Jim. She spotted him on the lawn by the pool and headed in that direction, her mind thinking of the one man she shouldn't think about. She smiled up at Jim and whispered in his ear. When he looked down at her, stunned, she only nodded at her suggestion.

Jim surveyed the crowd, instantly catching the eye of the pretty blond woman. Helen almost laughed when both of them blushed. Jim quickly looked away, then pulled out his wallet with a business card, wrote his private number on the back and handed it to Helen. Helen palmed the card and stuffed it into the waistband of her skirt so it would be safe until she could pass it along to Amanda.

The group was laughing about something Helen hadn't caught when she felt the tingles along her neck. She tried to shoo them away, but the tingles wouldn't go away. She looked around and froze. About twenty feet away was Alec and he didn't look happy. He was standing alone but when she looked at him, he moved toward their group.

"Good evening," several of the people gushed out, astounded that the head of their company would enter their group of employees.

"Good evening, Jim, Marty." Helen had to acknowledge that it was impressive of Alec to know everyone's names, even their wives and he greeted each of them with a façade of warmth. Until he came to Helen.

There was a definite coolness about his demeanor as he addressed her. "Helen. How have you been lately?" he asked, his dark eyes looking at her dangerously.

Helen took a deep breath. She'd been looking down when he'd spoken to the others hoping he'd just skip by her and be on his way but when he directly addressed her, there was nothing she could do but look up. It was worse than she'd thought. Alec in the office was one thing but here in his own domain with his tie off and the top buttons of his shirt undone, he looked incredible. Or maybe he always looked this magnificent and she was just putting parameters around him. She wasn't sure. "I'm fine," she replied, holding her breath.

"Caused any other minor catastrophes lately?" he asked with mock innocence.

Helen heard the sharp intake of someone's breath but ignored it. His question only angered her, since it was embarrassing Jim who wasn't sure which person he should defend. "Oh, you must be asking if I've humanized any part of your organization lately."

"Tomato, tomahto," he mimicked, changing the accent for the same word.

Her eyes flashed her anger at him but she wouldn't back down. "No, as a matter of fact. You should know by now that I've been avoiding all contact with Dionysius Corporation."

Alec's eyes skimmed to Jim, then back to her. "All evidence to the contrary."

She squared her shoulders and glared at him. "Actually, I didn't know that this was a company party. Jim forgot to mention that little detail to me," she ignored Jim's mumble of protest and continued at Alec. "If I'd known, you must be aware that I'd be on the other side of London now, enjoying a cheap cup of coffee and enjoying it much more than your excellent wine."

She must have known he wouldn't take that comment from her. He turned to Jim and smiled politely. "You'll have to excuse me, Jim. Your...date..." he hesitated over that word, obviously not liking it one bit, "and I have a difference of opinion we need to hash out."

He didn't wait for her to agree but simply took her elbow in his grip and pulled her along to a deserted part of the patio. When he stopped, she pulled her arm free and turned to face him. "Yes, there's all that charm you're so famous for. I recognize it now."

Alec gritted his teeth, not sure if he wanted to throttle the beauty standing in front of him or kiss her until neither one of them could think any longer. "You want charm?" he growled. "Then how about if you stop flirting with my staff and be honest with yourself."

She gasped. "I'm *not* flirting with your staff!"

His eyebrow went up with her declaration, silently challenging her assertion. "What would you call showing up here with a man who is trying to climb the corporate ladder? You're not exactly the good little wife sort, now are you?"

That hurt. "That's the worst thing you could say! Take it back!" she said through gritted teeth, one hand fisted at her side while the other one held onto her wine glass with a firm grip, trying desperately hard not to toss it in his face for that last insult.

Alec snarled at her. "Why should I?" he demanded and pulled Jim's card out of her skirt waist band, holding it up like a gauntlet. "Give him up, Helen. Or I'll fire him without any kind of recommendation. He'll never work in Europe again."

Helen snatched the card out of his hand and snapped, "You're horrible! I can't believe you'd even stoop so low as to fire someone in your company simply because I'm friends with him."

He leaned in closer, his anger almost palpable. He grabbed the hand that was still holding the business card aloft and leaned forward, his body language trying to intimidate her, bend her to his will. "Getting a man's private phone number constitutes more than just a friendship! Or are you so free with your wiles that you'll sleep with just about any man?"

She squared her shoulders and glared at him, furious with his arrogant attitude and his ungentlemanly comments which, as far as she could tell, were completely unprovoked. "You're out of line, Alec. And you're being horrible!" She pulled her hand out of his grip, thankful that he let her go. She started to walk away from him but he stopped her by grabbing her elbow and swinging her back to face him, tearing the card back out of her hand. "I'm not kidding, Helen. I never make idle threats."

"For your information, *Mr. Dionysius*," she slurred his name like an epithet a moment before grabbing the business card out of his hand again and putting it behind her back so he couldn't snatch it, "this phone number is not for me but for someone else. And I'll appreciate it if you'll stay out of my business in the future. I'll catch a cab home tonight."

Helen was so furious, she forgot to be circumspect about the plan she'd hatched a half hour ago. Instead, she walked over to Amanda, handed her the card and apologized. "Here," she said as the blond woman took the card, looking a little wary. "Jim's a great guy. He'll treat you well but don't hurt him," she said softly.

Without another word or a glance at anyone, she walked to the stairs, intent on leaving and never speaking to Alec again. She'd almost made it when she felt Alec's hand on her elbow. She didn't want to make a scene but she was too furious with him to accept his bullying techniques.

"Leave me alone," she whispered, glaring up at his handsome face and trying desperately to keep some space between their bodies. She couldn't get close to him or she'd... she didn't want to even think about what could happen if he touched her. She was angry with what he'd said, but her anger didn't seem to diminish her attraction for the awful man.

"I can't," he replied back through gritted teeth and moved her over to one of the other groups. He introduced her to several of his vice presidents and Helen was stunned when the charm she'd witnessed that first night reappeared. She kept stealing glances at him, wondering what had ticked him off earlier. She didn't care, she huffed and took another glass of wine, sipping it angrily. She kept trying to scoot away and add a little space between them, hoping she could escape and get home, get away from him but each time she tried, Alec foiled her plans by anticipating them and countering them. She spent the next three hours gritting her teeth and trying to escape, while at the same time, wishing her jelly-like knees would become stronger when he touched her casually, or that her eyes didn't stray so often to his firm mouth, wanting him to kiss her, feel his hands on her body.

She sipped her wine slowly, careful not to get drunk by switching to club soda later in the evening. That would only tip the odds in his favor and she definitely wasn't going to give him that much power over her. Each time she found her eyes on him, she pulled them away, knowing that her thoughts would also stray.

The crowd slowly thinned out but Helen wasn't aware of that. She stayed on the patio, ignoring the air that was cooling down as the sun set. It was still warm but she didn't notice. In an effort to counter his tingling touch and the heat that emanated from him while he kept her close by his side, she fueled her anger about his irritating manner. She was polite and interested in what anyone else had to say, but ignored him when he spoke.

Suddenly, she looked around and noticed that everyone else was gone and was startled. "I need to leave," she said when she caught him looking at her with an odd gleam in his eye. She set her glass down on a table and shivered. She could feel his eyes watching her, boring into her back.

"How are you going to get home, Helen?" he asked softly, the intimacy of the night closing in on them now that all the other guests had departed.

"I'll..." she wasn't really sure about that. Looking around, she realized that even Jim had left her. Then she remembered giving Amanda Jim's business card. "Did Jim and Amanda leave together?"

Alec's mouth frowned. "I believe so. You should give up on him. He wasn't right for you."

"I know that," she said in exasperation. "Why do you think I help the two of them get together?"

He looked at her curiously and walked forward. "You really aren't interested in Jim?" he asked.

"No."

He watched her for a moment before he finally accepted her answer. "Good. I'd hate to lose him. He's a good man."

Helen's mouth dropped open. "You really would have fired him? Just because he was dating me?"

"Yes."

"That's ridiculous."

He took a strand of her hair between his fingers, feeling the texture. "You're mine, Helen. The sooner you come to realize that, the better for both of us."

His words sent a shiver of tension, of excitement through her body and she was ashamed. She shook her head. "No, Alec. I can't. Nothing's changed."

He didn't say anything as he looked down at her, his eyes searching each of her features before he finally smiled. "Come," he said and took her hand in his. "You've barely eaten anything tonight and have only had a couple of glasses of wine. We'll eat in the library while the catering crew cleans up."

Helen couldn't deny that she was hungry. Famished actually. But that didn't mean she wanted to stay here with him. "I think it would be wiser for me to call a cab so I can go home."

He kept walking and the hand at the small of her back kept her moving as well. "Wiser probably, but not the best plan of action."

"Depends on your definition of 'best'," she replied.

He smiled down at her irritated, but flushed face. He liked having her here in his home and wasn't ready to relinquish her company. "My definition, of course, overrides yours," he chuckled.

Helen couldn't help it. She'd never met anyone so arrogant and yet so amazingly charming about it. "You're incorrigible," she said, trying and failing to smother her own laughter.

"Of course. Come along," he said and pulled her beside him. Along the way, he grabbed two plates and filled them up with the leftovers from the appetizers. Helen watched him, her mouth starting to water as he selected several different appetizers. "Don't forget those," she said, pointing to the small éclairs and other delicious looking pastries.

"Sweet tooth?" he asked.

"Big one," she replied with an unrepentant grin.

He chuckled at the excited expression on her face. "I'll have to remember that."

She laughed and shook her head in automatic denial. "Don't bother. I won't be around for another meal."

They left the patio and she followed him through the house, down a long hallway to a set of double doors which opened up to a large library. The room was three stories with books lining the walls from the floor to the ceiling, with two sets of balconies and strategically placed ladders so one could reach the higher books. "Good grief, Alec. Don't you do anything on a small scale?"

He laughed. "When it is required, of course."

"And you need all these books?" she asked, sitting down in a large leather chair and slipping off her shoes while he handed her a plate. He took off his jacket, tossing it over the back of the leather sofa and sat down across from her. "I like to read."

"Have you read all of them?" she teased.

He looked around. "I'm making my way through them."

She popped a cheese ball in her mouth. "That's admirable. What kind do you like the best?" she asked.

They discussed literature, pop culture, the current state of the education system and politics, each topic segueing into the next. It was almost midnight before Helen realized what time it was. She glanced at her watch, then sat up straight.

"Goodness, I'd better get home," she yawned. She couldn't believe how much she enjoyed talking with him, just being with him. It wasn't just his body that excited her, but also his mind which was swift and articulate. She wished she could find something about him she didn't like. Anything her mind could latch onto as a trouble issue and would allow her to think of him as only a friend, just like the other men in her past. Alec was dangerous on a level she just didn't know how to handle.

He'd already discarded his plate and both were sipping brandy. He put his empty snifter to the table and looked across at her. "Come here, Helen."

Helen tried to resist. She hesitated, seeing the gleam in his eye and knew what he wanted. Her mind told her to get up and leave, that he wouldn't stop her. But her body wouldn't comply. She'd been watching him all evening, talking, walking amongst his guests and generally just being the sexiest man alive. And now he wanted her in his arms and she knew he'd kiss her, and probably a lot more.

She should leave. She should just get up, slip her shoes on and walk out the door. It was the safer plan. It wouldn't lead to more knowledge of this dynamic, amazing man. But she wouldn't do it. Even as she licked her dry lips and stared across at his, thinking about his kisses, wondering what his touch would feel like and telling herself it would be emotional suicide to go to him, she knew that she was going to throw all caution to the wind and walk those few feet to him and feel him against her, know his kisses and revel in all the electrifying feelings he could spark within her.

She made one condition. "We can't have sex, Alec."

"Trust me," was all he would say. He didn't promise that she'd be safe, only to trust him.

She did.

Lifting her hand, she reached out and touched his. His hand closed over her small one and he pulled her gently towards him on the sofa.

Alec pulled her down so she was sitting in his lap. "Kiss me, Helen," he said but didn't wait for her to take the initiative. He pulled her close, his mouth covering hers, making her breathless as his mouth moved over hers, his tongue touching her lips, demanding and gaining entry.

When she pulled away, his mouth moved to her neck, his hands brushing against her waist, touching, gently caressing and making her wiggle underneath his touch. She desperately wanted more, but she refused to give in to that need.

After several long minutes of this torture, Alec pulled away and stood up, pulling her up with him. As he stared down into her eyes, he saw something there that made him nod with approval. "Now I'll take you home," he said and took her hand, leading her through his house to a limousine that was waiting out in the front.

The drive home was done in silence but Alec didn't relent on his sexual onslaught. His fingers holding her hand tickled her palm, making her stare down at their joined hands, wondering how such a light touch could make her breathing rapid, her heart accelerate and her body desperate to move closer to his, to become as close as possible.

"Alec…" she started to say but he stopped her.

"You're home," he said and stepped out of the car, reaching down to help her out as well. He led her up to her apartment and, at her doorway, kissed her gently but thoroughly, leaving her sighing, her eyes almost crossed with a desperate need to have him touch her more.

"Good night, Helen," he said softly before walking away from her.

Chapter 5

Helen woke up and stared at the wall. She was still exhausted, having woken up breathless twice during the night. She'd thrown off the covers and tried to calm down but the dream had been too vivid. She'd been making love to Alec in her dreams and she was still aching, desperate for him even now.

There was no getting away from Alec. He seemed to end up anywhere she was. Earlier in the week, he'd turned up at a photo shoot and took her out to lunch. Another day he met her in the park with a picnic lunch, then asked her about the people she'd photographed. When he went out of town for two days, he called and told her when he'd be back, asking her to meet him at the airport. When she said no, he told her to write down the date and time he was scheduled to land. And since it was his plane, he could be there anytime. "Meet me at the airport, Helen" he'd said again. And of course, silly woman that she was, she did. And was met with a huge bouquet of white roses and a mind numbing kiss, followed by a trip to a village fair where he took her on every ride available, even voting for the best pig and largest cow. Helen hated that she laughed hard at all the silly games they played but she hated even more that he was breaking down her resistance, showing her that he was really a nice guy underneath all that arrogance.

He called her house just as she was arriving home each night and told her he was taking her out to dinner. When she denied him, he resorted to telling her where he was taking her, tempting her with savory foods and amazing desserts. She wasn't gaining weight because she was too wound up the following day to eat, having been subjected to yet another sexual onslaught at the door to her apartment when he dropped her off.

After two weeks of this pressure, she wasn't sure if she was coming or going at times. Waking up after one of these evenings with Alec, she pushed the pillow over her face and screamed. She hoped she wasn't disturbing her neighbor but couldn't help it if she was. She didn't know what to do. She wanted Alec so much but she had a promise to her father and she had to keep it.

Helen threw back the covers and showered, changing into a pair of jeans and plain white tee-shirt. In her hair, she covered the top with an old scarf, gypsy style, then added several sets of pearls and a black leather belt. Feeling more like her old self again now that she was dressed, she grabbed her camera bag and left her apartment. She had a lot to do today.

Twelve hours later, she dragged herself back home, desperate for a long soak in the tub. She hadn't heard from Alec today and denied that she was disappointed. She wasn't addicted to him, she told herself as she dumped her bag down beside the door.

Looking through her refrigerator, she contemplated the contents. Nothing but a bottle of milk which was probably way past its prime, a brownish head of lettuce and one egg. The freezer wasn't any better but at least it contained some frozen meals. Accepting that she'd have to microwave something or go out, she pulled out the meal.

The phone rang.

She ignored it and slammed the door closed on the microwave.

It kept ringing. She glared at it until it stopped ringing and went to voice mail. After a moment, she walked over to her cell phone and pressed the button, replaying the message. "Helen, I know you're there. Call me back," Alec said, his deep voice challenging her, commanding her to do something she knew would be a bad idea.

She bit her lip and contemplated the idea. If she called him back, he'd take her out to dinner. Then he'd kiss her and drive her crazy with need, then leave her on her doorstep while his eyes demanded that she invite him in.

She turned away from the phone. The microwave dinged and she grew even more frustrated. Her cell phone pinged again, but this time, it was a text message. "*Helen, call me,*" he ordered.

She opened the microwave and stuck her fork into the still frozen pasta.

Another ping and she glanced down at the text message. "*Okay. I'll be out of town for three days. When I get back, we're going to talk. Be safe, Helen.*"

Helen turned to stare at the phone. Alec would be gone? For three whole days? The desolation that invaded her heart was painful and she looked around at her tiny apartment, feeling like the world had just tilted on its side and she couldn't regain her balance. Why hadn't she answered his call? If she had, Helen could have heard his voice for a few moments!

No! She would not be upset by that news! She would be fine without him. Great even. No problems, no frustration. She could get some sleep and develop some of these pictures.

Calling her mother, she scheduled a dinner with her, then two of her other friends. She was determined to not think about him at all. Or about how much she missed him.

If she thought about him during the next three days, it was only to hope that he was safe and not overworking. If she dreamed about him at night, she quickly gave herself a cold shower and pretended that everything was fine.

Four days later, Helen sighed with happiness. Another picture sold! The check in her hands wasn't much but the picture of the sunset she'd sold would show up in a prestigious travel magazine. She might not make a lot of money on that one, but she'd get lots of recognition. And it was all because of Alec. Well, his view, at any rate.

She stared at the check the whole way up the stairs to her apartment, almost dancing with excitement as she reviewed the name over and over again. This was the first time they'd ever accepted one of her pictures although she'd submitted several before. Even as she looked at the evidence, she still couldn't believe that she'd finally broken through and had one accepted! It was like a special birthday and Christmas all wrapped up in one.

Dumping her heavy camera bag beside the door, she danced through her tiny apartment to the kitchen. Tonight, she didn't even notice the chipped, blue linoleum she'd asked her landlord to repair about ten times, or the water leaks in the corner of the ceiling. Tonight, all she could see was the travel magazine check and her heart couldn't calm down. This was monumental.

She pulled out the bottle of white wine she'd been savoring the previous few days. Although it had been out and exposed to oxygen, which diminishes the taste, the quality of the wine was such that it didn't matter. At least not to her. She didn't have the money to throw away. Since she enjoyed a good bottle of wine so much but didn't have the money to get rid of an already opened bottle if she couldn't drink it that same night, she accepted the slightly tarnished taste. It was still immensely enjoyable.

She changed into a pair of shorts and a tank top, immediately feeling relief from the heat. The air conditioner in her apartment wasn't working very well so it never really cooled down. She plopped down onto the comfortable but well worn, orange couch she'd found at a second hand shop and breathed a sigh of relief, taking a slow, wonderful sip of her wine. It was crisp and pungent and alerted all her senses that an explosion of flavor was about to hit. Then wham! Her tongue experienced the oak, the fruit and the touch of chocolate. Amazing! And oh, so satisfying.

She held the check up, blocking out the soft, yellow color of the walls she'd painted the previous year to enhance the orange couch and stared once again at the travel magazine name. She really owed Alec a thank you, her conscience told her. He'd had his office invaded, his staff corralled and his evening disrupted. The least she could do was send him a note letting him know that his patience was rewarded.

She wouldn't even need to see him, she thought, her mind working a mile a minute. If she just got him a gift, some small token of her appreciation for his patience, she could simply give it to Mick and he could make sure it got to Alec. That wouldn't be cheating on her promise not to see him anymore, would it?

Boy, she missed...No! she stopped herself. No, no, no! She couldn't think about how much she missed him. Even arguing with him. That was completely inappropriate. It had been four days and she wouldn't do anything about it.

She needed to just get him the thank you gift, then stop thinking about him, get on with her life.

She took another sip of wine and thought about how perfect her plan was. Her mother would be proud of her creativity and her father would be glad she hadn't broken her promise or put herself into a situation where she might be tempted.

She was completely in control, she smiled. No worries if she dropped off a thank you gift and she could just move on after that. There would be no reason to think about him ever again. She could even see Edna when she wanted and not need to ask about Alec. Helen knew that Edna and her mother had formed a fast friendship and were having lunch together next week but Helen wouldn't need to ask how Alec was, if he was still angry with her or find out what had happened while he was out of town. Or if he was okay or if he was getting enough sleep and not working too hard....

But what could she get him? The man had so much money, he could buy just about anything he wanted. She took another sip of wine and contemplated what might be an adequate gift for what he'd done for her.

The flavor burst once more, giving her a sense of contentment and pleasure but her mind was still a blank on a gift. Perhaps one of her pictures? Maybe in a nice frame? She could even give him the sunset picture. That was the whole reason for the gift, wasn't it?

And a bottle of wine!

Helen sat up, suddenly feeling as if the world were back to spinning properly on the axis she'd set in motion. Yes! A bottle of wine and the sunset picture would be perfect!

She savored the rest of her glass of wine slowly, thinking of all the possibilities when it came to wine and then her mind touched on the perfect bottle.

An hour later, Helen stared at the bottle, hoping inspiration would come to her. She'd gone to her discount supplier, the one down the street that had a store which looked more like a hole in the wall than an actual retail market but he sold some of the best wines, even if they were sometimes pricy. The bottle was her favorite red wine, a full bodied pinot grigio that she suspected Alec would appreciate. It had taken all one hundred dollars she'd received for the picture but the sale wasn't really about the money. It was about recognition and a breakthrough. She didn't usually spend a hundred dollars on one bottle of wine but what could she do when buying a bottle of wine for a zillionaire? She had to spend a little more simply because he wouldn't care for something less than the best, she knew.

She bit her lip, considering the nights they'd gone out to dinner. She'd recognized the labels of the other wines and they'd all been excellent but there was no way she could afford those. This one, her favorite, was all she could afford but now that she'd bought it, what should she write on the note? The words had to create the perfect balance between graciousness so he understood how important this event was, and finality so he knew that she couldn't see him anymore.

"Alec," she wrote on the light green stationary she had on hand for notes, "Thank you so much for allowing me to invade your office. Just so you know it wasn't in vain, I'm proud to let you know that one of the pictures will be published in one of the best travel magazines. Thank you for the opportunity. In gratitude, please accept this bottle of wine in appreciation."

She re-read the note then nodded with satisfaction. Putting it into a darker green envelope along with a smaller copy of the sunset picture, she sealed it and tied it to the bottle of wine with a special ribbon.

She worked hard the next day and her camera bag was especially heavy since it was carrying the bottle of wine. Helen calculated she could make it to her first photo shoot, drop off the bottle during her lunch and then still make it to her afternoon appointment. It was such a simple plan, what could possibly go wrong?

Chapter 6

Alec stormed out of the airport, irritated at the whole world. He wasn't really angry at the world but at one, cute, irritating, sexy female with eyes that wouldn't leave his head. He wanted her. And not just her body, he'd realized grimly as he was driven from the airport back to his head-quarters two days after his anticipated return. It irritated him that he wanted to talk to her even before he wanted to check in with his office.

When had he ever wanted to talk to a woman? Women served one purpose and one purpose only. They were interesting creatures; soft, lovely, full of interesting curves but not interesting conversation.

And why the hell hadn't she tried to call him? Even once, dam-mit! He'd held off calling her during the whole trip only to see if she'd call him first and now he wanted nothing more than to hear her voice and see the laughter in her gorgeous green eyes.

Why in the world would he want to be around her, argue with her, laugh with her and hear her laugh with him? That was unheard of, he thought with burning irritation. He turned on his laptop and forced himself to concentrate on the current acquisition. It would be a simple one, he knew, but strategic. The target company was vulnerable in places the owner didn't even realize. By the time the markets opened up in three hours in Athens, everything would be all over. The man had left a key part of his small empire vulnerable and so he deserved to lose it all. No man should leave himself open to attack. Keeping his family and possessions safe was the ultimate goal for a man and Alec knew that lesson better than anyone else. He had found more vulnerabilities in other companies than anyone and knew how to protect his own.

Unfortunately, even the sweeping success in business hadn't been able to distract him from thoughts of the sexy, impertinent and ever so outrageous woman. As he typed in instructions to one of his vice presidents, he couldn't stop thinking about Helen.

As he shut down the computer, he shook his head and erased the possibility of talk. He didn't really want to talk to her except whatever words it would take to lure her into his bed. That was all he needed, he told himself. He could bed her, enjoy her and be done with her so he could move on. He wasn't used to having to work this hard to get what he wanted when it came to women. They threw their lovely bodies in his direction constantly and all he had to do was pick which one interested him at the moment and for however long his interest lasted. Then he moved on, knowing that there was always another woman to conquer.

Maybe that was it as well, he thought as he walked swiftly through the lobby of his headquarters building. Maybe she was just one of those challenges he needed to conquer. Perhaps he'd been thinking about her too much and once he actually got her into bed, he'd discover that she wasn't as alluring or intriguing as he'd been anticipating all along.

That had to be it, he thought. She was just a mystery, a challenge that he'd been working through. Just like any other business deal he'd decided to conquer, his mind had fixated on her and, since she was more of a challenge than the other women he'd bedded, he was simply working through the details. Alec always won whatever he went after and Helen was one of those resisting issues he needed to conquer.

"Good afternoon, Edna. Is the contract ready?" he asked as he walked past her desk.

Edna snapped to attention as soon as he walked through the door, eager to please him since he'd been in such a good mood lately. Well, actually he'd been a bit of a beast in the past two days, but she'd attributed that to his schedule getting off of the expected path. "The newest version is printed out on your desk with the revisions you asked for," she said, following him into his office.

Alec stopped short, his eyes narrowing in on the bottle on his desk. "What's that?" he demanded but he already knew. Helen. The burning inside him increased as he realized that she'd been thinking about him as well.

Edna was quick to explain, a huge grin spreading across her face. "Helen dropped it off along with the picture she sold. There's a note that goes along with the wine." Edna knew that he'd been seeing Helen regularly and, in Edna's opinion, she was the main reason for her boss's current good humor. Life had been so nice for the past several weeks.

Alec picked up the bottle and read the label, frowning. "Helen bought this for me?" he asked, remembering how she'd only had nine dollars in her purse the first night he'd taken her out to dinner, and how she lived in a minuscule apartment. How could she afford a bottle of wine this expensive?

Edna shook her head. "I'm sorry, Mr. Dionysius, but I didn't read the note. I'm not sure what it's for."

He picked up the envelope. His eyes were drawn to the picture and he was stunned by the intensity of colors she'd been able to capture from his balcony. He looked at the picture for a long moment, absorbing the sunset, relishing the fact that Helen had taken it. That alone made the picture much more astounding.

"When did she drop this off?" he asked, his eyes skimming the note.

"I think it was about noon. Is there a problem?" she asked.

He dropped the note onto his desk but propped the photo against his light, knowing he'd want to see it later on. He picked up the bottle and examined the label, his eyes growing concerned. "This is from our vineyard," he explained absently.

Edna smiled tentatively and wondered about the look in his eyes. It wasn't one she'd seen before. If she had to put a name it, she would say he was actually confused but that was impossible. Edna had been working for this man for more than five years and she'd never known him to even be indecisive, much less confused. "I thought so. Why is that a problem?" she asked. "Don't you like the wine you're producing?"

"It's excellent wine," he murmured. "Call Jimmy and tell him to meet me out front."

He walked back out of his office, completely ignoring the work that he needed to be resolved this afternoon.

Fifteen minutes later, Alec was knocking loudly on Helen's door. The sound was a little harder than perhaps was needed but he was impatient to talk to her and find out about the bottle of wine. And to see her. It had been too long. He'd wanted to call her while he was away even after he'd resolved to wait for her to call him first, but he wasn't sure his frustration level could take the long distance communication. He wanted her and it was becoming painful. He was going to have to stop this torture and finalize the issues with Helen. He'd find out why she was so resistant to become intimate and then work out a plan to get her over her fears of the sexual act. There was no way either of them could continue with the way things were going.

It took her a few seconds longer than he could wait so when the door opened with her smiling face, Alec was furious.

"Dammit Helen, did you even know who was knocking?" he demanded, pushing his way into her apartment and slamming the door on his body guards.

Helen's shocked expression turned to anger. "What are you talking about?" she asked, backing up quickly in an effort to keep from getting too close.

He wouldn't give her space though. He knew exactly what she was doing and closed the distance between their bodies. After having been denied her company for the previous four days, he wanted nothing separating them. And he wanted satisfaction on several points. "You opened the door without finding out who was knocking. What if it had been someone other than me?"

"Someone who might stalk me and make me nervous, you mean?" she asked pointedly.

He wanted to smile at her wit but held back. "I mean, someone who might cause you harm. Helen, you're a female living alone in the city. You should know better than to open your door so trustingly."

"You're being silly!" she challenged. "Stop stalking me, Alec! Stay where you are."

She reached up to push her hand against his chest, hoping to stop him but he ignored her feeble attempts. He continued, pressing her back so she was cornered. "Why? I want answers."

She glared at him, wishing her heart didn't accelerate and that the man didn't smell so good. Hadn't he just gotten off a plane? Shouldn't he be exhausted and all rumpled? But no! He had to look glorious and rested and as fresh as if he'd just woken up, showered and changed this morning. He simply wasn't human, she reminded herself. "I didn't look because I was expecting my neighbor. She's baking and she usually forgets something from the store."

That stopped him in his tracks. "Baking?"

She stomped her foot in exasperation and desperation to put some space between them. "Yes, you oaf! Can't you smell the cookies?"

Alec stopped and sniffed the air. He could actually smell something baking now that he stopped for a moment. He'd missed it initially, having thoughts only of getting Helen alone and naked. The smells he now could decipher made his mouth water but also calmed his temper slightly.

"Fine. I'll accept that. But you're getting a peep hole installed. You shouldn't ever open the door unless you know exactly who is on the other side."

Helen's arms crossed over her chest. "That would be lovely, Alec. Believe me, if I'd known you were on the other side, I definitely wouldn't have opened the door."

Alec almost smiled at her impertinence. Didn't she realize who she was talking to? He could buy this ridiculous excuse for a building, tear down the door and force her out of here. Then he could very happily have her ensconced in one of the apartments he kept around the world. The idea appealed intensely right at the moment but he had other priorities that wouldn't leave his mind.

"Next question," he started off.

"I don't remember a first question," she retorted.

"Where did you get this bottle of wine?" he demanded, holding up the bottle of pinot grigio.

"At a store," she replied, lifting her head slightly. Her lip wobbled slightly and she was terrified that she would lose control. She was barely hanging onto what was left of it now and she needed him to leave as quickly as possible. "Look, if you don't like it, you just have to say so. It's one of my favorites but I can't afford it very often. I'm sorry if I picked something you don't like but you don't have to be so ungracious about it."

"Which store?" he asked, ignoring her second part of the statement. "How can you afford this wine?"

She sighed in exasperation. "Alec, I'm not so poor that I can't afford a hundred pounds of wine for a friend in gratitude."

He leaned into her, his hand wrapping around her waist and pulling her forward, flush against his body. "First of all, I'm not your friend. I'm going to be your lover which is significantly different," he growled out. "And secondly," he said before she could protest his first statement, "this bottle of wine happens to cost over a thousand pounds. And from what I can see, you definitely can't afford that kind of money, even if it is for your future lover."

Helen's mind had started whirling at his initial contact but the second part of his statement also blew her away. "It isn't a thousand pounds! That wine is very good but it only cost a hundred pounds. That's why I like it so much. You can't get that kind of quality for so little now."

Alec pulled her closer. "Helen, please don't try and tell me how much this wine is. I can guarantee that it is well over one thousand pounds."

Her hands reached up to push against his chest in a futile attempt to get some space between their bodies but in the end, her hands were holding him instead of pushing him away. "Just because you pay too much for something doesn't mean the rest of us can't find a bargain."

He reigned in his temper with difficulty. "Helen," he gritted out, "I know exactly how much this wine sells for."

That got her anger back up and she wrenched out of his arms, taking several deep breaths before turning back to face him. "Everywhere?" she challenged. "Alec, you can't know what every vendor sells a bottle of wine for. I'm not as business savvy as you are but isn't there something called discounts?"

"Not that big of one. Honest business people don't sell a product at a ninety percent loss."

"Maybe my source just has cheaper sources."

"Maybe your source is stealing the product."

She stared at him for a long moment, wondering what he meant. When his comment broke through her dumbfounded mind, she inhaled sharply. Helen shook her head adamantly. "No way. I know the guy personally and he's very nice. He doesn't steal anything. He has four kids and a wife to support. He wouldn't put them at risk."

Alec was stunned at her naiveté. "Helen, just give me his name and I'll investigate."

She considered his request for a long moment but then thought better of it. "No, Alec. You don't know everything and you'll just make Arnold have to get an expensive lawyer to defend himself against your accusations. I won't let that happen to him. If you don't have enough to do with your own companies, then find some other person to bother. I won't help you there."

He leaned over her in his anger. "This *is* one of my businesses," he enunciated slowly.

Helen's mouth dropped open. "Impossible!"

"Possible," he countered. "Not only do I own this particular vineyard, I also own the distribution company that has exclusive rights to several vineyards. So yes, I know exactly what I'm talking about when I say that this particular bottle of wine is well over one thousand pounds."

Helen was stumped. She wasn't sure how to answer him anymore. His assertion completely knocked the power out of her argument and she backed down slightly and said, "Oh, well. I...um...yes, perhaps you do know how much the bottle is."

"And the name of the person who sold it to you?" he demanded, still looming over her.

Helen's eyes shot back up to his, worried now. "No, Alec. I wasn't kidding about Arnold's family. If he's selling me wine at a deep discount, then you'll just come in and mess up his whole business. That wouldn't be fair to Arnold or his wife. I won't do that to a friend."

Alec held back but it was getting more and more difficult. "Helen, have you ever seen the man's family?" he demanded.

She looked at him warily, wondering what he was trying to get at. "Well, no. But..."

"So you've only heard stories about his wife and four children?"

"Yes....but..."

"And isn't it possible that maybe one person of your acquaintance might have lied, ever so slightly just to gain your trust?" he demanded relentlessly.

She thought about poor Arnold and his tiny little store a block away. She'd never seen his family but she'd seen pictures his kids had drawn and thought she was a good judge of character. If someone was a thief, she'd know it, she told herself. "No!" she answered, her back stiffening. "Arnold isn't like that!"

Alec grew more and more furious when she continued to defend a man who was most likely a criminal selling black market products. "Helen, give me his name!" he almost yelled.

Her hands were balled into fists at her sides and she shook her head, refusing to give him the information. "No. I don't betray my friends!"

He couldn't restrain his temper any longer. He pulled her roughly into his arms and glared down at her. "What about me, Helen? What if someone is swindling me?"

That scored a bull's eye. She closed her eyes, not allowing herself to look at him. It was bad enough that her body was starting to melt in his arms, just his touch making her weak in the knees. "I think you need to leave."

"Why?"

"So I can go find Arnold and warn him that some zillionaire businessman needs more money and is on the rampage looking for him," she yelled back, trying to push out of his arms.

"You're not going to find him, Helen," he said, his mind going blank with the jealousy eating at him with every one of her words. "I'll destroy any man who touches you," he said a moment before his mouth covered hers.

Helen tried to resist him. And if he'd continued the brutal attack, she might have stood a tiny chance of doing so. As his mouth crushed hers, she pushed against his shoulders, punching his rock hard arms. In response, he lifted her up and pressed her back against the wall, his chest pressing against her breasts and she gasped at the contact. When his hands moved down her body, cupping her bottom, she wiggled, her mind no longer functioning. Then his hands moved from her bottom, to her legs, bringing each of her knees up, indicating that her legs should wrap around his hips. That was the end of her resistance. When she felt his hardness against her warmth, her arms stopped battling against him. Instead, they fought to bring him closer. Her eyes closed and her mouth opened, her lips and tongue seeking his, finding him and tasting him, kissing him with everything inside of her. All the passion she'd been denying for so long was finally released and she reveled in his return desire.

She was uncontrollable. Her fingers delved into his hair, touching the softness, the only part of this man that wasn't hard. When her fingers needed more stimulation, they ventured to the skin on his neck, feeling the textures and the heat, then needing more. Coming around his neck, she pulled at his tie, tearing it off his neck. As soon as he was free of that cumbersome material, her fingers worked on the buttons of his shirt, tearing them open in her desperate need to feel him, to touch him and seek out more of his warmth.

She didn't realize that he was doing the same thing. All she knew was that her mind had finished trying to cope with all the thousands of messages zinging to her brain and had shut down. Her body was on overload and reveling in it. She wanted more of him. When his fingers released the clasp on her bra, she arched back, feeling his fingers against her bare skin. There was a moment of blackness but she didn't realize he'd just pulled her shirt over her head. Only that the intensity had increased. His hands were covering her breasts and she gasped, her fingers stilling in their excursion over his chest to revel in the feeling of another person touching her breast. No man had ever touched her there. None had been allowed beyond a kiss and Alec's touches and kisses weren't even in the same mediocre level as the other men she'd dated. Alec was beyond anything she'd ever imagined.

The world tilted and suddenly, she was on her bed, with Alec looming over her. He ripped off his shirt and tossed it somewhere behind him, then came back down over her. She inhaled sharply when she felt his hard, powerful chest against her bare breasts but didn't slow down. Her hands, now free of the irritating restrictions his shirt had imposed, roamed freely, her nails biting into his muscles and shoulders when his mouth covered her nipple. She cried out and arched her back, giving him better access, wordlessly begging him to continue and he accepted the invitation. His teeth nibbled, his tongue soothed, then his lips sucked until she was a quivering mass of need. "Alec, can't.....take anymore," she gasped out, her hips lifting to press into his, unsure of what was going on, only knowing that the feelings that seemed to be ripping her apart were coalescing in her core.

He lifted up once again and she opened startled eyes to see him. But she couldn't focus. All she saw was his intense gaze working on her belt, then his long fingers pulling her jeans off. She sighed with pleasure and lifted her arms, begging him to come back to her. He took only long enough to pull off his own pants and boxers, ripping off her underwear before coming back to her.

Helen's legs parted instinctively for him, her legs wrapping around his waist.

Helen felt his hardness nudge at her core and shook her head, not sure if she could take anymore. "Alec, please, I can't..." then she felt him enter her. It was slow and gradual and her eyes opened, amazed at the incredible feeling. She looked up at him, saw the sweat on his forehead and understood how hard it was for him to take this slowly.

Her hands reached up and touched his cheek and his mouth turned into the caress, kissing the palm of her hand. "I can't slow down Helen," he apologized and pushed all the way into her.

Helen felt the pain instantly, but it was quickly gone. She arched against him, her body immediately accommodating his size. She felt whole, as if this was what she was made for, what she'd been waiting for her whole life. Her arms and legs wrapped around him, her body arching into his touch, silently giving him the signal that she was okay.

Alec looked down at the beauty in his arms and couldn't believe how perfect she felt. She was so tight, so incredible, so amazing that he wanted to both push into her, his body clamoring for release, but also move slowly, take her higher and make this first time perfect for her.

When she wrapped her arms around him, he moved in and out, watching her face for any sign that she was still in pain but her mouth formed an "o" of surprise and Alec breathed a sigh of relief. He moved again and felt her body shift slightly, then lift up against his. Taking it slowly, he moved, gradually increasing the tempo, driving her insane. He could feel her hands, her nails, her body urging him to go faster but he didn't and when her body tightened against his, her screams of satisfaction drove him over the edge. Moments later, he found his own release, his arms pulling her legs higher and he couldn't believe how long his orgasm lasted. It was as if every muscle in his body was completely replete and he collapsed on top of her.

Several moments later, he felt something on his shoulder. Rolling onto his back and taking her with him, he realized that it was Helen. She was kissing his shoulder, her hands fluttering about his arms.

He pulled her hair back, running his fingers through her hair and stared up at the ceiling as she turned her head, resting her cheek against his chest. And damn, that felt extremely nice!

Why wasn't he getting up? Why was he just laying here, enjoying the aftermath of the most incredible sex he'd ever had? He never stayed after sex. He always made sure the woman found release first so he wouldn't feel guilty when he climaxed and then showered. He hated the touchy-feely part of after sex.

So why did this feel so nice? Why did he shift his body slightly so her soft kisses would reach more of him?

The questions were too numerous and too difficult to answer. And he felt too good. He didn't want to think about how or why this time was different. He just wanted to enjoy it.

Rolling her onto her back once again, he looked down at her face, his body hardening when he saw the look of contentment on her pretty, satisfied features.

"You look like a cat who finally got the mouse," he commented, a moment before his mouth kissed her neck.

She laughed and tilted her head to give him better access. Helen's body was still tingling from moments before but when his tongue reached out and teased her neck, she wiggled underneath him. "Alec, I'm not sure I can do that again," she started to say but his mouth covered hers, stopping whatever she was about to say.

"I'm sure," he said when he lifted his head. His mouth then moved down to cover her incredible breasts, taking the pink nipple in his mouth and savoring not only the taste but the sounds she made and the way her body responded to him.

He slowly made his way down her stomach, kissing and teasing her stomach. She couldn't believe how nice this felt and closed her eyes as his mouth teased her stomach, her thigh.

He moved even lower and Helen shifted, trying to stop him from doing...that! But the man only chuckled, the deep, sexy sound causing her body to shiver with anticipation, Helen was too focused on that, and how nice those soft kisses felt, that she forgot to stop him again.

Helen almost shrieked when his mouth covered her. She wasn't ignorant. She knew what men and women did in the bedroom, having read magazines and books about the subject. But nothing had prepared her for this kind of sensation. When his tongue darted out, she sat up and considered pulling him away. The feeling was too intense, making her weak and hot and shaky all at the same time. But then when his mouth moved into place and his finger slipped inside her, she fell back against the pillows and arched into his mouth. It was like she was his puppet and he called all the shots. His tongue dipped and she gasped, his mouth covered her and she twisted, his finger moved and she arched. The dance continued for several long, amazing minutes before she exploded, her mind reeling and her fingers clenching in his hair. Then slowly, she floated back down to earth, her lungs trying desperately to get enough air but nothing was enough.

Alec laughed, exulting in the fact that she was finally his, once and for all, completely and irrevocably his. And he didn't care to analyze why that fact was so important to him. It just was and he was enjoying her too much to care.

He entered her slowly, watching her facial features which changed from smiling contentment and feline satisfaction to surprise, and followed by her body needing what his now needed. The two of them rode the crest, feeling the heat and both writhing with need, and he wrapped his arms around her as they both reached the crescendo together.

"Impossible," she whispered, holding him tightly.

Alec silently agreed but wouldn't let his arms relax. He felt her grip on him ease slightly and looked down at her as she drifted into sleep. Alec moved to her side and watched, content to simply watch her face which was still smiling in her sleep.

Glancing at the clock, he wasn't surprised to see that it was already after ten o'clock. He'd been here for over five hours and hadn't even thought about work once. Even now, remembering all the details he needed to get tied up, he couldn't stir himself enough to care. Instead, he pulled Helen against him and put his head down on the pillow, allowing her to sleep for a bit before he woke her up for more of the same. Because although he'd had her twice, he already felt his body stirring for the next time. No, this woman definitely wasn't going to be only one night.

Chapter 7

The obnoxious sound wouldn't go away. Helen snuggled deeper into her bed, feeling warm and comfortable. The sound came again. Her brain was trying to tell her something but she didn't want to wake up enough to figure it out.

She stretched and curled up next to the warmth, trying to move the pillow under her head so she could smother the sound. But that was too much effort so she gave up, sighing with pleasure. The bed moved underneath her and Helen held onto to whatever was solid. Unfortunately, the only thing solid near her was a large male chest. Her fingers pulled away as if they'd been burned.

The chuckle under her ear startled her the rest of the way out of her sleepy haze. "You're not going to get out of this bed if you continue to do that," Alec muttered, his lips nuzzling her neck and making her shiver.

Helen gasped, her hands moving along his shoulders and memories of the previous night came back to her. In vivid detail.

"Don't go shy on my now, my little wildcat," he murmured when he felt her stiffen.

"Alec!" she gasped when his hand moved up her back, hitting a sensitive spot on her spine that sent shivers along her body.

"I know, I found that spot early this morning," he said, smiling as he moved down her body once again, his intent obvious.

"Wait!" she said, pulling at his hair.

Alec sighed and looked up at her. "What's wrong, my dear?" he asked, grinning as his hands continued where she'd stopped his mouth.

"No, please Alec, we can't..." she started to say but then the ringing started again.

Alec's eyes quickly found the culprit. "My phone. It must be

72

important if they're calling back," he said, his voice husky as his body moved on the tiny bed to retrieve his cell phone that had fallen out of his jacket pocket during the rush to eliminate clothing the previous night. "Just a moment," he said and flipped open the phone to answer it.

Helen tried to find the sheet and pull it over her nakedness but she wasn't exactly sure where it was. It didn't matter anyway since Alec rolled onto his back, pulling her on top of him so her entire body was flush with his while he answered the phone.

His expression was amused at her embarrassed and harassed features as she held onto his chest in her effort to balance herself. When he heard the caller's message though, his expression changed. Suddenly, he was all business. His eyes looked at the ceiling as he listened, his jaw tense. "Understand. Thank you for the information. I'll be there immediately."

He closed the phone and Helen grabbed hold while Alec rolled over once again, gently tucking her underneath him. "I'm sorry, Helen. Something's come up. I have an emergency I need to attend to." He kissed her gently before standing up and pulling on his clothes rapidly.

"What's wrong?" she asked, her embarrassment overridden by her concern for his grim expression. "Is everything okay?"

"I don't know," he replied, buttoning his shirt. "I have to leave for a few days but I'll be back. I promise."

Helen tried to hide her disappointment and sat up, pulling her pillow in front of her to hide herself. "It must be horrible."

"Definitely not what I was expecting," he replied, pulling on his shoes. He stuffed his tie in a pocket and patted the other pockets.

Alec couldn't believe his luck. He was livid that something so ridiculous could happen and on the morning when he'd finally gotten this gorgeous woman to be with him. All he wanted to do was to climb back into bed with her and ignore the crisis that had emerged. But his sense of duty wouldn't let him.

He was just about to rush out the door, his security detail already alerted to the situation and standing by, when he looked down at Helen. She was curled at the top of the tiny bed, a pillow covering her chest and her long, sexy legs curled underneath her. He could tell that this was not the ideal "morning after". If he had it his way, he would make love to her one more time, carry her into the shower and soothe every ache he suspected she was feeling, then take her out for a long, leisurely breakfast. Then back to his place for more of the same.

He cursed under his breath when his body reacted to the image in his mind. Dammit, how could he want her after a night of the most incredible sex he'd ever had? How could his body even think along those lines?

Alec stopped rushing, realizing that she was fighting tears and sat down next to her. She was twenty-four years old and had just lost her virginity. This must be a monumental morning for her and he wasn't exactly sure what to say. "Helen…"

She put a hand to his arm, stopping whatever he'd been about to say. "No, Alec. Please, just go," she said, biting her lower lip and turning her head away. "You have something to do and I…" she took a deep breath, obviously trying to get her emotions under control, "I need some time alone."

Alec didn't like that. He didn't like the fact that she was fighting back tears or the unreasonable need to take her into his arms and make the world right again for her. He wasn't even sure what was wrong, since everything he'd been feeling ten minutes ago was extremely right.

"I'll make it up to you, Helen. I promise."

Helen nodded but she wouldn't look at him. That, more than anything, bothered him. He put a finger under her chin, turning her face so he could look at her, but her eyes were closed. He gently touched her lips and heard her cry but didn't understand it. "Helen, talk to me. What's wrong?"

Helen wasn't sure if she wanted to pound her fists into his chest or curl up on his lap and demand that he fix everything for her. She was too devastated to think properly at this moment though. She was angry with herself for letting this happen. She'd broken her vow to her father and nothing could make it right again, no matter how much she wished it could.

"You have to go," she said and closed her eyes, refusing to look at him. She didn't want to see his kindness. Or pity. She wasn't sure which would be worse. All she wanted was to be alone so she could figure out how she was going to deal with this.

She knew that she shouldn't feel guilty about having sex. It was a natural, instinctive, healthy activity. And the vow she'd made to her father…that had all been part of a "purity culture" that should have been banished decades ago. But…she'd promised her father. At the time, it had seemed like such and easy promise to make. And it had been! Until Alec had entered her world.

"Helen…" he started to say but she shook her head and pushed against his shoulders.

"Please, Alec. I just need to be alone and you have a crisis."

Alec stood up but he wasn't happy about this. "We'll talk about this when I get back. I shouldn't be gone more than three days."

"Fine," she said, swallowing painfully. In her mind, she knew she'd be unavailable for his calls. She promised herself she wouldn't ever see him again, knowing that she couldn't control herself where he was concerned. And she couldn't do that to her father. She was too ashamed already. She wouldn't add insult to the situation by becoming Alec's mistress.

Alec sighed and reluctantly left her apartment. Once he'd closed the door, he had the sudden urge to go back to her, tell her to pack a bag and come with him. But that was ridiculous. She'd be bored in Greece, knowing what he had to deal with. He wouldn't have any time for her which would only make the situation worse. There was nothing worse than a bored lover.

Of course, a part of him wouldn't mind a bored Helen, just so long as she was with him.

Where that thought came from, he had no idea so he pushed it aside and walked quickly to the bank of elevators. He found his security detail behind him, not even realizing that they'd been standing sentry outside the door.

"Is the plane standing by?" he snapped out. For the first time in his life, he was irritated that his business life was imposing on his personal life.

"Yes, sir. The plane is already fueled and there's a departure slot in thirty minutes."

"Fine," he said, taking a deep breath.

Chapter 8

Helen listened for the footsteps outside her apartment door, waiting until they were far away before she curled up in a ball and released her emotions. She found the sheet and covered herself as the tears streamed down her face. Curled at the bottom of her bed, she reviewed the evening in her mind, trying to find a point when she could have turned things around, stopped the actual finale from happening. But as the scenes flitted through her mind from one to the next, she acknowledged that the only way she could have stopped her downfall was to have avoided Alec completely. And if she were completely honest with herself, she admitted that she hadn't worked hard enough to accomplish that.

How could she have allowed this to happen? With Alec of all people! The man hadn't said the words, but she knew that he wasn't the kind of man who would want a long term relationship. And Helen wasn't mistress material. She wouldn't, couldn't, become available to a man, waiting for him to come to her.

She was so ashamed that she'd ignored her warnings. And embarrassed. She'd heard about the morning after but had never believed it would be this horrible. Humiliating!

The phone ringing beside her bed brought her out of her misery for a moment. Sniffing, she picked up the phone, hoping she didn't sound like she was crying. With her luck lately, it would be her mother calling who would immediately know something was wrong. Knowing her mother, she'd be over here within the hour, demanding to know everything and congratulating her on finally experiencing sex for the first time.

"Hello?" she said through the phone.

"Hello?" a heavily accented voice replied. "Is this Ms. Helen Miller?"

"Yes," Helen said, sitting up in the bed and immediately sensing that this wouldn't be a pleasant phone call. "Who is this?"

"This is the Athens Hospital. I'm sorry to tell you this news over the phone but the distance...." The stranger started to say.

Helen's whole body tensed. "Athens? What's wrong? Is my father okay?"

The stranger hesitated. "Is your father Petros Miller?" she asked carefully.

"Yes, Yes. What's wrong?" Helen asked, terrified now. "What's happened?"

"Your father has had a heart attack, ma'am. He's stable at the moment but is asking to see you."

A sob tore from her throat. "No!" she cried out. "Please tell me you've made a mistake. It can't be my father!"

The woman's voice became more firm in an attempt to break through Helen's panic. "Mr. Miller is stable but he is asking to see you. Can I tell him you will arrive?"

"Yes!" Helen gasped. "Yes, please. I'll call back as soon as possible with the flight information. Please tell him I'm on my way and that I love him. Tell him I'm coming!" she cried out, her mind frantically trying to figure out all the arrangements she'd need to make. She took down the hospital's contact information, promising to call the nurse back as soon as she'd booked a flight.

Helen hung up the phone immediately and logged onto her computer. With fingers that fumbled over almost every key, she searched for the earliest flight she could get out of London to Athens. She didn't care about money in this circumstance. She had a credit card her father had given her for emergencies and this definitely qualified as one. She'd never used it for anything else, but right now, this wasn't about her being independent and finding her way in the world on her own skills and resources. This was about getting to her father as soon as possible. After several minutes, she finally found a flight that would leave in an hour.

She called the hospital while shoving clothes into her suitcase, uncaring if they were folded or not. She didn't carry much, knowing she'd left a whole closet full of clothes at her father's house. They were a different sort, her father not liking her gypsy style very much. When she was with him, she tried to make him happy by wearing clothes that were a little more conservative and to his liking. So she only needed underwear and the basics until she arrived at his house and the hospital.

She quickly showered and pulled on a pair of jeans and a tee-shirt, slipping her feet into the first thing she could find but grateful that they were comfortable shoes for the long flight. Grabbing her suitcase, purse and passport, she rushed out the door.

After a grueling five hour flight and a chaotic taxi ride to the hospital, Helen finally arrived at the hospital and found out from the nurse's station that her father was still in the intensive care unit. She was emotionally and physically exhausted after a night of very little sleep and a plane ride made more difficult because of her guilt over her father's health, sure that she'd brought this on by her behavior of the previous night with Alec.

With trepidation, she walked down the hallway the nurse indicated and pushed open the door. When she saw her father, with all the tubes and monitors coming out of his arms, the breathing tube in his nose and something else down his throat, she could no longer hold back the tears that had been held at bay during the horrible trip.

Slowly moving towards the bed, she watched her father, terrified that if she moved too quickly, she might startle him and create another heart attack.

"Oh, Papa!" she whispered, unaware of the tears rolling down her cheeks and dropping onto the white bed sheets. She took his cold hand and sat down in the only chair in the room. Careful not to touch any of the tubes or monitors, she took his hand gently in hers, terrified at the lack of strength. He looked gray and his lips were almost completely white. She couldn't believe the expression on his face. It was as if he was fighting but couldn't come out of his sleep to put up a good battle front.

"I'm so sorry," she wept, bringing his hand to her cheek as she watched his chest rise and fall. "I've let you down. I broke my promise to you and I'm so sorry," she whispered, wishing he was awake so he could hear her apology. "I've let you down and I've shamed the family name and I promise I'll never see him again. I'm so sorry you had to find out about it but I promise, Papa, I'll never speak to him, never see him again."

She squeezed his fingers, wishing she could give him some of her strength. "Papa, please don't die on me. I promise from now on I'll be the epitome of a good Greek daughter. Just like you always wanted! I'll meet all the men you'd like, I'll seriously consider whichever man you think is best for me, just please don't leave me. I need you so much! I need your guidance and I'm so confused but I promise I'll never see him again. Just fight this, Ppa!"

The nurses rushed into the room, speaking rapidly in Greek but Helen, fluent in the language herself since she'd grown up speaking it whenever she was with her father, understood what they were telling her. Thankfully it was only vital signs they wanted to monitor but she listened, trying to hear anything that might tell her what was going on. And then she looked up...

Chapter 9

Alec was just about to leave the hospital room when the door started opening. He knew he had no right to be here. He wasn't family but he had the power to overcome the hospital rules. Since it was Alec's actions which had put the man into the hospital, he guessed it was only right that he see if there was anything he could do to help. He'd flown out here this morning after hearing about the man's heart attack. When Alec had started the strategy that would eventually take the man's ships out of his control, Alec hadn't known that the man would be so angry that a heart attack would result.

When the black, curly head of hair appeared in his line of vision through the doorway, Alec thought he was seeing things simply because Helen had been on his mind so much lately. He'd deeply regretted the necessity of leaving her this morning and had set in motion plans that would expedite his current trip, wanting to get back to her as quickly as possible. Something hadn't been right when he'd left but he couldn't think what had gone wrong.

Except him leaving.

No woman liked to feel rushed after a night of sex. Especially after last night's incredible sex, he acknowledged. Helen deserved better, he thought. It had been her first time and she deserved, needed, to be treated better. She'd given him a gift and in return, he'd left her the morning after, rushing out without an explanation.

As he watched, thinking he was losing his mind, the rest of her sexy body appeared, in jeans that hugged her cute bottom perfectly and a tee shirt that emphasized her voluptuous curves and tiny waist. She wasn't wearing any makeup which, in his mind, only made her more beautiful. She had a natural beauty that stunned him, being used to women that wouldn't dare show their un-made up faces to anyone, much less in his presence.

Her words at the bed of this man astounded him. She was pleading with the man who was obviously her father. Alec couldn't speak for a long moment, his mind working through the details. He'd known that the man had a daughter but the reports from his investigators hadn't gone into details about the daughter's identity. Alec had been going after the man's company, not his family. This was just business and if the man couldn't take care of his business, then he didn't deserve to run it, in Alec's mind. Nothing personal, just business.

Now, seeing his Helen weeping beside the man's bed, holding his hand, it suddenly became personal. Alec's mind tried to process this new piece of information, but he couldn't put the pieces together just yet.

Then her words sunk in. What had she promised? Who was she never going to see? Was it him?

Hell no!

There wasn't any way he'd let her follow through on that promise! And just who the hell was her father going to marry her off to? His Helen was going to become a "good Greek daughter"? How was she going to accomplish that, he wondered. Good Greek daughters married and had babies but his Helen wasn't going to marry anyone! She was his!

She continued to weep and hold her father's hand, swearing over and over again that she'd never see "him" again but Alec's mind went into high gear. If Helen was upset about her father's heart attack, he could make it right. If her father would demand that she marry, then he'd make sure Helen married him! There was no way he'd allow her to move to another man's arms. She'd been a thorn in his side for several weeks now but she was *his* thorn. And he'd be damned if he'd let her marry some other man.

Nurses moved into the room at that moment, obviously preparing to take his vital statistics and Helen moved out of the way. As she moved, their eyes caught and he wouldn't let her look away.

"What are you doing here?" Helen demanded, looking across the miserably clinical intensive care room at the man who had been on her mind for the past several hours. She'd sworn just five seconds ago that she'd never see Alec again, but here he was, looking magnificent and gloriously strong and all she wanted to do was throw herself into his arms and cry out her heartache for what she'd done to her father, beg him to heal her father with whatever powers he had at his disposal.

The nurse shushed them into silence. "I think your father is waking up," the older one warned.

Helen tried to ignore Alec as she moved to her father's bedside. "Papa?" she said, seeing his eyes flutter softly. "Oh, Papa!" she gasped when she finally saw him try to smile. Taking his hand, she squeezed it gently and was thrilled when she felt him squeeze her hand back. It was barely there, but she'd felt it and her heart soared with gratitude that, at least for the moment, he was here with her.

The nurse smiled and called the doctor. For the next thirty minutes, there was a flurry of activity. Helen was asked to leave the room so they could examine her father, promising that the doctor would give her more information about his condition as soon as they were finished. Helen reluctantly left his bedside and walked across the hall to the waiting area, worry and fear tempering her mood but she was so grateful to have Alec right behind her.

Moving across the room to the linoleum chairs, she turned to face him, avoiding the temptation to fly into his arms and sob out her misery and shame. "What are you doing here?" she asked, curious at first.

"This was the phone call I received this morning."

She was confused. "You know my father? How?"

Alec moved further into the room but since it was empty except for the two of them, he was open with her. "I have business interests with your father," he said carefully, not wanting to reveal too much about the takeover he'd instituted several months ago which had most likely created the pressure on the older man's heart and created this heath crisis. He was pretty sure Helen would be furious with him at his actions and right now, he needed to figure out what was going on.

She slumped into a chair and sighed heavily. "So you and my father work together. I'm sure that's good in some way," she said softly. Sitting was good. She was a little more able to resist throwing herself into his arms.

"Helen, what's wrong?" he asked and sat down next to her, taking her cold hand into his warm one. "Tell me what you were talking about with your father before the nurses came into the room."

She immediately jumped up and moved away from him, crossing her arms over her chest. "I can't," she said, shaking her head back and forth. "Please Alec, don't come near me."

Alec looked at her grimly. "That's not possible, Helen. Not after last night."

"No!" she practically shouted, then ran her fingers through her hair. "It's because of last night that my father's here." She looked around, frantic now. "Last night can't ever happen again!"

Alec raised one eyebrow. "I don't think your first statement is entirely accurate," he replied, thinking about the takeover he'd finalized only hours before news of her father's heart attack had reached him but he said nothing of that at the moment, knowing that Helen wouldn't be able to handle that news right now. "But even so, how are you going to do that?" he demanded.

Taking a deep breath, obviously struggling for patience, she sat back down again but not near him. "A while ago, I told you that I'd made a promise to someone, remember?"

That reminder, added to the fact that she'd just told him she'd never sleep with him again, made his temper rise dramatically.

Hiding his feelings as best he could, he replied, "Yes, vividly."

His mind quickly calculated several different conversations, plus the information he'd gathered about her father and added several things together. "It was to another man but you wouldn't explain it to me. From what I overheard in the other room, I'm guessing your father is the man to whom you made this promise?" he asked cryptically.

"Yes," she said, nodding warily. She looked into his dark eyes, filled with intelligence but which were also hard and uncompromising. He meant everything he said and the only way he would understand her position is if she told him everything. "I promised him I wouldn't shame the family. And I failed in my promise to him." It was hot outside, but the fear for her father left her chilled to the bone. She walked over to the window, wrapping her arms around herself in a feeble attempt to gain some warmth.

"How did you do that?"

She turned back to face him, smiling wryly in an attempt at humor but the tears threatening to spill over her lashes defeated her endeavor. "I used to try and explain this to my boyfriends in the past but they never understood. But they weren't Greek." She laughed and looked out the window. "I'm not sure why I never made the connection between your last name and your heritage but I guess that's silly of me. You're very Greek so I'm assuming you'll understand what I'm about to tell you."

He could see the pain and shame in her eyes and wanted to walk to her, comfort her, pull her into his arms and tell her that he could make everything right again. But he could tell that any form of affection might break down what little control she had left. So instead, he said, "I'm Greek, yes, if that's what you're trying to explain."

She nodded and looked at him as if she'd never seen him before. Now that he was here in Greece, she could definitely see the olive skin, dark hair and the noble features. She felt silly for not grasping his lineage before now. "Yes. So you'll respect the issue a little more than the others."

Alec took a deep breath, striving for patience. "Then explain it to me, because right now, you're not making any sense."

She nodded. "Yes, I'm sorry." She started pacing around the room once again, unable to determine if sitting or pacing helped deal with this conversation better.

"You see, almost ten years ago, something happened in our family. My cousin was beautiful and witty and vivacious and she was so much fun to be around. She was three years older than I was and at seventeen, she got pregnant. Her father was furious and the boy who was with her wouldn't marry her. Papa had the power to destroy the boy's family, but not the power to force him to marry his niece." She took a deep breath and stared out the window, not really seeing anything since the view was of the parking lot, but in her mind, she was picturing the scenes in her father's house, the awful fights, the crying from her cousin, whom Helen had idolized as a young teenager, and all the relatives arguing over what should happen. It had been a very difficult period in their family's history. "We all knew something was wrong, but by the time she got up the nerve to tell her mother and father, my uncle had already guessed and was furious."

Alec grimaced, having heard tales like that before. Greek fathers, especially those in the smaller villages were extremely protective of their daughters for this very reason. "A teenage pregnancy sounds bad, but not completely unheard of. It happens."

Helen didn't smile. "I know it happens, but at the time, I was fourteen and all I could understand was that the whole family was furious with my cousin who was too young to bear that kind of burden. My uncle lived in a small village near the coast. The villagers have very conservative values so after Amelia got pregnant, everyone found out and they scorned her. A village that had always been warm and welcoming had turned into a horrible place to visit."

"What happened?" he asked, but he already knew.

Helen's body shivered at the memory and she closed her eyes, wishing she could shut out the pain of the past as well as the present as easily. "Amelia lost the baby. It was stillborn. There were fights in the family during her entire pregnancy, everyone yelled at each other, everyone accusing the other, blaming anyone for what had happened. The villagers would cross the street whenever Amelia walked past, she cried a lot, her father stopped speaking to her and she came to live with us. Papa would never turn family away and his house was much bigger so it wasn't an issue. But Amelia was so ashamed every day."

"What happened after she lost the baby?" he asked softly, afraid of where this story was going.

"She healed physically, but as soon as she could, she left Papa's house. She and her father still don't speak to this day although she's happily married with three children now. She lives in Italy and won't come back to Greece for any reason."

"And the promise?" he prompted.

She didn't explain for a long moment, battling her tears.

Finally, she got her emotions back under control. But Helen looked out the window as she explained. "When the fighting started, Papa pulled me into his study and sat me down. He explained all about sex and how babies were made although I'd already understood the concept. Then he asked me to promise him that I would never have sex until I was married. He made me promise never to bring shame down on the family and create that kind of anger." She buried her face in her hands as her shame overwhelmed her. "And I did. Last night, I broke my promise to my father, a man who has only given me everything kind of advantage, always had a warm hug and a kind heart, who listened to me, no matter what was going on in my life." She turned tear-wet eyes up to Alec. "He's so kind and generous and loving. He took Amelia in and never hurt her, never blamed her, and all he's asked of me was to not bring shame on the family. And now I've not only broken my promise, but he somehow found out and I've almost killed him with the news!"

Helen's body doubled over with the shame and emotion building up inside her and she couldn't seem to stop crying. Even when Alec pulled her into his arms, she was too overwrought to pull away. "What have I done?" she sobbed, accepting his comfort by wrapping her arms around his shoulders.

Alec let her cry, knowing she wouldn't hear anything he said anyway. He saw the nurse indicate that they should come back into the room and he pulled away from her, handing her a handkerchief. "Come along. Your father is asking for you." He let her wipe away the tears, then put a finger under her chin so she was looking at him. "Everything will be fine, Helen. I'll make it so. Come along," he said and took her hand to lead her back into the room before she could deny him. "But you have to understand one thing," he said and waited for her to look at him before continuing. "What we did last night did not cause your father's heart attack. There were other circumstances, of which you're not aware," he said.

Alec watched, knowing that she didn't understand. She couldn't at this point, being too overwrought to think about anything but her guilt and trying to figure out how to make her father well again. "Come, let's go speak with your father," he urged, leading her down the short hallway back to her father's room once more.

Helen followed, too eager to see her father and talk to him again to pull back from Alec. "Papa?" she said as she entered the room once again. She was relieved to see that the tube from his throat was gone and he was sitting up slightly, but still very weak. The color in his face was horrible, but at least he was conscious. That had to be a good sign, she told herself.

He smiled at her and weakly lifted his hand to hers. "You are here. I thought I was dreaming it," he said weakly.

Helen walked over to the side of the bed, trying to keep her eyes from all the scary monitors and their beeping, taking his hand in hers and holding it in both of hers. "Yes. I flew out here as soon as I heard the news. How are you feeling?" she asked, bringing his hand to her cheek.

He grimaced in response to her question. "I thought I dreamed that you were apologizing for something. What a silly man I am," he smiled. His voice was weak but he shook his head as much as the wires and tubes would allow. "You would never bring shame down upon me, would you Helen? You're a wonderful daughter and I'm glad you're here with me. I'm just sorry it is in this way and not a happy vacation for both of us, eh?"

Helen tried to hide her surprise but thankfully, he floated off to sleep once again. The nurse explained that he would do that off and on for the next forty-eight hours and Helen shouldn't be concerned.

"Have you eaten?" Alec asked once the nurse was gone.

Helen shook her head, swallowing her misery. "I'm not hungry," she replied, her eyes never leaving her father's face. She didn't want to look away, afraid she'd see Alec and want things she couldn't have anymore.

"Helen, we need to talk. Come outside again."

She shook her head. "No Alec. I can't do that. I'm fine right here."

The soft, feminine voice snapped both of them around to the door of the hospital room. "What's going on in here?" Helen's mother said, looking haggard and worried as she took in her daughter's red, tear stained face and her husband's gray pallor. "Helen, fill me in. I just arrived from the airport. What happened?"

"Mother!" Helen gasped, then snapped out of her horror and rushed over to hug her mother. "Goodness! I'm so sorry I didn't call you. I just got on a plane and rushed out here."

"I know dear," Elisia soothed, hugging her daughter back fiercely.

"I heard from Edna what happened. Thank goodness she made the connection between that old goat who went and had a silly heart attack and my husband," she said, glaring at the man sleeping on the hospital bed.

Helen saw the fear in her mother's eyes behind the glare and reacted to it. "The doctor was just in here and they've already taken the tube out of his throat so he's breathing on his own now."

Her mother's sharp eyes looked over her husband critically, assessing each line of his face and gray hair on his head before moving down to view the rest of his body covered in a white hospital gown and white sheets with tubes and monitors. "What else? What caused this to happen? I thought he was healthy but you know how he works way too many hours," she said, admonishing the man even though he was unable to defend himself. Her reproach was softened by her taking his hand gently.

Helen watched in shock as her mother leaned over to the bed and gently laid her other hand on his weathered face, kissing each cheek. She saw the love and a huge lump of emotion formed in her throat. She'd never understood why they hadn't divorced but now, seeing the love shining through her mother's eyes, Helen finally grasped that they couldn't divorce. They were still too much in love.

Helen smiled slightly when her mother turned back to face her, waiting for an answer. Knowing that her parents' crazy relationship worked for them, she shrugged off her concern and questions in deference to the immediacy of relieving her mother's mind. "I haven't spoken to the doctor yet, mother. How about if we both go and get more information?"

Elisia turned to look at Alec. "Good afternoon, Mr. Dionysius. How are you?" she asked, her voice not the normal warm tones. Helen was surprised to find a slight chill to her mother's voice.

"Mother?" she asked, confused by the anger she sensed coming from her normally very friendly mother.

Elisia shook her head and glanced down, sighing deeply. "I'm sorry. I'm judging your boyfriend on hearsay and I know that's not fair." She glanced back to Alec who was standing at the end of the bed. "And you're here with Helen and that counts for a lot." Her smile and the more relaxed shoulders told Helen that, whatever she had against Alec, it wouldn't last much longer. Elisia was too much of a people person to let grudges stand in the way. Besides, she was also a diehard converter. Was that also the reason she'd never divorced Helen's father? Did Elisia still think she could bring him around to her way of living?

Helen smiled softly, her respect for her mother growing exponentially in that moment.

"I'll always be there for Helen," Alec said, his eyes conveying some meaning Helen didn't really understand right at the moment but she suspected that there was a profound communication that she needed to grasp... quickly.

Needing to distract her mother from Alec's unspoken message, she touched her softly on the shoulder. "Um...mother, how about if we go find out more about father's condition and see what he needs?" she suggested, wanting to get as far away from Alec as possible. And get her mother away from him. Her mother's eyes had softened, become curious with Alec's comment.

Elisia snapped out of her thoughts and came back to the present. Blinking, she looked back down at her husband and sighed, patting his hand gently. "Yes. I think that would be a very good idea."

The two of them went out into the hallway and immediately found the doctor who was discussing treatment at the nurses' station. The doctor explained the heart attack and the treatment he was recommending, adding that the patient was recovering much more quickly than he had anticipated.

He smiled reassuringly at both of them. "In fact, if he continues to progress like this, I think we can move him out of intensive care by tomorrow morning."

Helen sighed with relief. "Thank goodness!" she said, hugging her mother before turning back to the doctor. "What can we do to help his recovery?"

"His heart is still weak so don't bring any business to him. He has to have no worries about anything. Once he's out of the hospital in about a week or two, depending on his progress, then he'll need physical therapy. He'll still need to take things slowly and with an absolute stress-free environment, which means no worries, no work pressures."

Elisia nodded her head. "Understand. I'll make sure it happens. What else?"

The doctor looked at Elisia for a long moment, then smiled. "I guess if anyone can slow that man down it will be you, am I correct?"

Elisia's determined expression showed her answer. "That old goat, you mean?" Her eyes were twinkling with mischief so the doctor didn't take her insult to heart. "Yes, he'll slow down. Don't you worry about that at all."

Helen laughed, hugging her mother's shoulders. "You're going to be horrible to him, aren't you?"

"You bet," Elisia said, nodding firmly. "He's going to live if I have to tie him down to do it. I didn't wait all these years for him to come to his senses only for him to die on me before he admits that I'm right!"

Helen didn't understand her mother's comment, but the two of them were already walking back into the hospital room. She noticed that Alec slipped out, returning several minutes later with cups of coffee for both of them. Throughout the day, he was in and out of the room, ensuring both Helen and Elisia had food, chairs, coffee, water and snacks as well as any other comfort he could provide.

Helen didn't realize the passage of time until Alec lifted her into his arms, starling her out of a light sleep. She woke with a sore back and snuggled into his arms. "Where are you taking me?" she yawned.

"You're going to sleep in a bed tonight," he said firmly and carried her down the hallway, exiting through a door and ducking into the back of a limousine. He put her onto the seat carefully, kissing her gently on her forehead before stepping back again. "Stay here, I'm going to get your mother," he said.

A feminine voice from behind him said, "I'm not leaving his side," she said and her eyes were hard and unyielding. "Take Helen home and come pick me up in the morning. I'll shower and change clothes once she's back here to be with him while I'm gone."

Alec eyed her carefully before finally nodding. "Fine. I'll see you early tomorrow morning with food and you'll eat before I escort you to my place to shower."

Elisia nodded, then turned back to the hospital so she could return to her husband's side.

Alec got into the back and nodded to the driver before pulling Helen back into his arms. He was only partially mollified when she easily came to him, snuggling against his chest. Once she was settled on his lap, he curled an arm around her waist and considered all that he needed to do. The list was long, but he had several staff members he could delegate the tasks to. He would just need to be strategic and careful.

When the limousine pulled into an underground parking garage, he lifted Helen into his arms, holding her while the private elevator whisked them to the penthouse. There, he carried her into his bedroom and slowly pulled her jeans and tee shirt off. Gritting his teeth, he unhooked her bra, then pulled one of his own shirts on over her.

Once she was tucked in, the sheets pulled over her slender body, his own clothes removed, he slipped under the sheets next to her, pulling her against him. Moments later, they were both asleep.

Chapter 10

Helen woke feeling as if something were wrong. Hadn't she had this warm, cozy feeling before? Her mind, still groggy from sleep, was slow to sort out the details of the night before. Why was she so sore? And warm? She snuggled down into the warmth, knowing instinctively that something that felt this good had to be bad. And she didn't want to find out the bad. She didn't want to remember. Her mind knew that something horrible was trying to come to the surface and she just didn't want to think about it now.

Her toes were cold and she moved them to the warmth. Her back was all toasty but she wanted to feel the same on the front of her. Pulling the blankets closer, she pressed against the heat.

The groan woke her almost instantly. Her eyes popped open and the heavy arm that had been resting against her waist pulled her more tightly against that heat source. "Don't move, Helen," Alec's deep voice said against her ear.

Helen stiffened. Again? Hadn't she woken like this yesterday morning? And then.... "Papa!"

Instantly, Helen sat up in bed, pushing her hair out of her eyes. Looking behind her, she spotted Alec in the dim morning light. "What are you doing here again?"

Alec rubbed his face, then ran his fingers through his hair before letting his hands drop by his side, looking at her with amusement. "I know you were tired last night but it's hard to believe you can't remember anything."

Helen bit her lower lip, her mind running through the last thing she remembered. "I know I fell asleep in the chair next to my father's hospital bed. But I don't remember how I got here."

Alec smiled ruefully. "In deference to your father who is probably waiting for you by now, I won't tease you about that comment." He sat up and tossed the sheets off of him, then walked unashamedly naked across the expanse of the large, beautifully decorated bedroom to the black marble bathroom while he said, "I brought you back here so you could get a good night's sleep. Nothing happened last night," he assured her. "Your suitcase has been delivered. It's at the end of the bed. Why don't you hop into the shower first?"

Helen held the sheet to her chest but her eyes were glued to the man's broad shoulders and perfect butt. How could a man so high up in the business world find the time to be so athletic? He was perfect, she thought, her mouth dry as she watched him disappear into the bathroom.

Shaking her head to get rid of the image, she looked down and wondered how she came to be wearing a large man's shirt. Glaring at the now empty doorway, she suspected that it had been Alec that was responsible for her current state of dress. Or undress.

She waited several moments after he disappeared, just to make sure he wouldn't catch her in such a vulnerable state, then threw back the sheet and hurried across the room. Catching a glimpse of herself in a large mirror over one of the dressers, she gasped at how she looked. Her hair was completely mussed and her cheeks were rosy. If it weren't for the dark circles under her eyes, she might look like she'd been making love all night instead of tossing and turning with worry about losing her father.

Actually, she paused mid-stride as she turned away from the mirror, her dreams hadn't been about losing her father last night. He'd definitely been in them, but...she nibbled at her lower lip, her mind concentrating on what had actually happened in her dream. She wasn't positive what had happened, but she knew that Alec had been in them, and he'd been at the hospital, strong for her, supporting her.

Sighing, she pushed thoughts of her dreams out of the way as she searched out the bathroom. She didn't have time for little things like analyzing her dreams. She had to get moving, get back to her father. He was probably asking about her and she didn't want to keep him waiting.

She had to confess, Helen told herself. Oh, she'd told him the whole story yesterday just as soon as she'd arrived, crying out her grief and guilt at her behavior. But he'd been unconscious at the time, so that confession didn't really count.

She stepped into the bathroom, glad that it was miraculously free. She wasn't sure where Alec had disappeared, but suspected that he'd gone through the other door. Where that led to, she wasn't going to find out.

The shower was heavenly. She couldn't believe how nice the water was and how the heat melted some of the tension of the day before. She didn't linger though. She was afraid to be away from her father for too long. She worried that she might miss something if she weren't right by his side.

While she was showering, Alec must have gone to another bathroom because he was already showered and shaved by the time she stepped out of the bathroom, a fluffy white towel wrapped around his lean waist, showing off his washboard stomach and making her shiver with excitement.

Not the time, she told herself and looked away.

"Um...where are my clothes?" she asked nervously, securing the large towel around her body as best she could. She'd love to have a robe, or even better, a very dowdy outfit right about now, especially when he turned to face her, seeing what she wasn't wearing and his eyes flared. Helen could see the desire all the way across the room and hated the blush that stole up her neck and into her cheeks.

"While you were showering, my housekeeper unpacked for you. They're in the closet," he said, pointing to another door, but said nothing about the fact that she was in his bedroom with only a towel wrapped around her.

Helen walked carefully over to the door, holding the towel in place. She was terrified that it would fall and reveal everything and she wasn't able to walk around naked as casually as....Oh no! Alec just pulled off his towel and was following her into the closet.

"What are you doing?" she gasped, backing up against the wall. Her eyes slipped to his chest, and lower, but then she squeezed her eyes shut.

She heard Alec's deep chuckle but didn't dare open her eyes. "Helen, you've seen, and more importantly, felt, everything so I'm not sure why you're being so shy now. You certainly weren't shy the previous night."

"No!" she gasped and turned around. "You don't understand. My father's in the hospital because of me. I did this to him!"

There was a long silence and Helen could feel his eyes on her. He didn't touch her, but she knew that he was trying to work out what she'd just said. "What the hell are you talking about?" he demanded.

Her eyes popped open and she was relieved to note that he'd pulled on a pair of stretchy boxers. They didn't hide anything, but the cotton material was better than nakedness.

"My promise! Remember?" she implored. "I let him down and somehow he found out. I've obviously hurt him so deeply by what we did together that I shamed him and caused his heart attack." Taking a deep breath, she shook her head and squared her shoulders with determination. "I can't let him down again."

Alec sighed and came closer, apparently unaware of his nakedness and the effect it was having on her. "Helen, listen carefully to me. Your father was in business and with that comes a lot of stress. Your father didn't find out about our night together and he won't, unless you tell him. That's up to you." He pulled her into his arms and held her gently, relieved when she didn't try to pull away. "Helen, you said you'd promised him that you wouldn't have sex until you were married, right?"

Helen nodded, feeling her cheek brush against the hair against his chest and liking it, loving the way he smelled and the strong arms that held her, soothing her, one hand rubbing up and down her spine and slightly massaging her tense neck muscles. "Yes. He always said that he wanted me to be the kind of woman that men respected."

"I respect you, Helen. And we're getting married." His tone would brook no argument, but that wasn't unusual. He was used to setting down commands and having people following them instantly and without question.

All the tension was instantly back and her spine stiffened as her mind absorbed his words. When she finally understood, her brain shifting into high gear and comprehension filled in the rest. Immediately, she struggled against him, wanting to get away, to shove him farther from her and out of her reality. "No!" she said with a vengeance.

"Excuse me?" he asked, his voice calm and deadly. "We're getting married, Helen. Just accept it."

She sputtered at his audacity and shook her head, pulling down the first pair of jeans she encountered from a hanger. "I won't! And there's really nothing you can say that will make me marry you. The idea is ridiculous," she snapped and stomped out of the closet, grabbing a white tee-shirt as she went.

Standing in the middle of the masculine bedroom, she was now stumped. She had outer clothes but Helen had no idea where his household staff had stored her underwear. She thought about putting on her jeans without underwear, but she just couldn't do it.

Alec walked out, buttoning a pair of soft jeans himself, leaving the top button undone while he searched for a shirt.

"That's not fair," she gasped, her eyes watching him as he casually walked out of the closet.

"I'm sorry?" he asked, stopping right in front of her and looking down into her troubled eyes. "I'm getting dressed, just as you are. What, in this particular instance, is not fair except for the fact that you're denying me my rights to marry you."

Helen's mouth fell open. "You're rights?!" She couldn't fathom what he was talking about. "What rights am I denying you?"

"You had sex with me two nights ago. According to the promise you gave your father, that was implicit agreement that you would marry me," he explained as if that were the most logical comment anyone had ever made. Fisting his hands on his lean hips, he glared down at her.

Helen sputtered for a moment, then gathered her wits. "There were no assumptions made. Anything you assumed, you did on your own and I won't be responsible for the warped way your mind works."

He took a step closer to her and, with one hand, he snapped the towel out of her hands. "What...?" she gasped and tried to take a step back but he captured her with his strong hands. "You can't..." she started to say but he stopped her completely by covering her mouth with his own, his tongue invading and forcing her to kiss him back. She resisted for maybe half a second before giving in to the desire to touch and feel and kiss and taste. There was no getting out of it, she wanted this man desperately.

When he felt her melt in his arms, he pulled away and looked down into her desire drugged eyes. "You'll marry me, Helen. Or I'll tell your father what we've done and he'll force you to marry me."

Without another word, he walked away from her, grabbing a shirt from a drawer as he headed towards the doorway. "Breakfast is on the terrace. Be ready in five minutes so we can eat quickly and tell your father the happy news."

Helen stared at the now closed doorway, her confusion and anger so strong, she couldn't form a coherent thought. He was demanding that she marry him? He was an absolute bastard! How could he? He was using her promise to her father to...to...! She wasn't going to marry the man! She couldn't! He was just...this whole situations was wrong! How odd, and very....traditional.

Chapter 11

Helen rushed through the hospital doors, both trying to get to her father's bedside but also needing to escape from Alec's presence. Since seeing him naked this morning, experiencing his kiss and then left wanting...she couldn't get the image out of her mind. She wanted him and felt as if she were betraying her father by those feelings.

She'd finally found her underwear and pulled on her clothes roughly, applied a smattering of makeup and then rushed out to find the terrace so she could confront him about his demands. But when she'd finally found the terrace, he was on the phone, speaking in German and Helen simply poured herself some coffee and grabbed a pastry before sitting down to glare at him.

He got off the phone moments after she arrived but didn't give her a chance to discuss the marriage issue. Instead, he gave her an update on her father, quickly transferring her energy away from an argument with him and changing to fear for her father despite Alec's reassurance that her father had improved significantly overnight.

"Good morning, Papa!" she said, with a bright, cheerful voice that she definitely wasn't feeling inside. "How are you feeling?" she asked, bending over and kissing his cheek, noting that he really did look much better today. At least his lips weren't blue and his face didn't appear as gray. There was even a slight tinge of color in his upper cheeks.

"Wonderful," he said, smiling weakly as he accepted her kiss, patting her on the hand in return. "You look refreshed," he said, his stern eyes taking in the high color of her face and the sparkle in her eyes.

Helen turned away from his too-knowing look and pulled the uncomfortable looking hospital chair closer to the bed so she could sit next to him and still hold his hand. "I am," she agreed with a falsely cheerful voice. "What's the news? Have the doctor's been by to visit yet this morning?"

Before he could answer, her mother stepped into the room, carrying three cups of coffee. While she was handing them out to Helen and Alec, she smiled down at Petros, a great deal of love shining through her eyes with that look. "He's being moved to a regular room today. His progress has been great over the last twelve hours."

Helen was so relieved, she slouched down on the plastic chair, blowing out a sigh. She took a bracing sip of the coffee and didn't cringe at how awful the brew was. She was only comparing it to the delicious, rich coffee she'd had less than an hour ago with Alec and this stuff was borderline toxic, she thought.

"So when might you be released from the hospital?" she asked, putting the cup of coffee off to the side.

"Helen, I need to speak with your father alone," Alec interrupted, his eyes hard and absolute, challenging her to defy him.

Helen had been ignoring him since they'd arrived at the hospital, not wanting to even acknowledge his presence or the bomb he'd dropped on her earlier this morning. But with his words, she looked over at him, knowing what he wanted to discuss and not liking it one little bit. Her fears escalating with the understanding that he was going to tell her father the exact opposite of what she wanted. "No, Alec. There's nothing you need to say to my father in private."

Elisia looked from her daughter to the man standing firmly at the end of the bed. She must have understood that something momentous was about to happen and stepped into the fray. "Helen, I need some help with something. Come along, dear."

Helen shook her head. "No! Alec has nothing to say to Papa," she announced firmly, her mouth set in grim lines while her arms were crossed over her chest, defiantly denying Alec his time alone with her father.

Alec didn't reply, but simply stared at her, glaring right back at her. Helen tried to hold his gaze but couldn't. She looked away first but was still shaking her head. "No, Alec. This is a family matter. Thank you for being here initially, but we're fine," she said, praying he'd take the hint and leave them all alone.

Without taking his eyes off of Helen, he said, "Elisia, would you mind taking Helen down to the waiting room? I have business to discuss with Petros."

Helen shook her head, but when her mother took her arm, she pulled against leaving the room. "Don't do it, Alec," she pleaded. "This isn't right. You and I need to talk more. This isn't the solution."

"You've already said all there is to say about the subject this morning. I have your answer," Alec said with a grim expression.

She had no alternative but to allow herself to follow her mother. Looking down at her father, Helen noted his confusion and concern, and she just prayed that Alec wouldn't say anything that would cause her father to regress.

Helen paced in the waiting room for five minutes before she couldn't take it any longer. "He can't do this," she said to her mother and slipped out of the door. Getting back into the hospital room was easy since they were already moving her father down the hallway to a private room.

Alec watched her from the doorway. "It's done," he said before she could provide any other comments to her father. "We're getting married, Helen."

"No!" she exclaimed, gripping the doorway to the waiting room. She felt the world sway and instantly, Alec was at her side, holding her steady. "Why?" she asked weakly. "Why did you do that?"

"It's done," he replied firmly, pulling her out of the way. "You're father has already agreed to my suit."

Helen caught her father's eye and shook her head. "Why not?" he asked patiently.

"Because..." she started to say but Alec crossed his arms over his chest, daring her to counter his claim.

"I....we...just don't....do well together," she finished lamely.

"We 'did well' enough on Wednesday," he countered.

Helen gasped at the reminder. "Don't!"

"I will," he challenged.

"You won't!'

His smile showed no mercy. "Don't challenge me on this Helen. You won't like the consequences."

She glared at him. "You wouldn't!"

"I will. Set a date!"

"No."

"Petros, the reason..."

"Fine!" Helen yelled. Pushing her fingers through her hair, she frantically tried to find an alternative. "But not until my father is out of the hospital."

Alec smiled as if he'd won a huge point. "Good enough. The day your father is released will be our wedding day. Make a list of anyone you want to invite," and handed her a note pad and pen from the nurse's station.

Helen grabbed the note pad and stormed out of the room, furious with him for pushing her into a corner like this.

How could he? This was intolerable. She couldn't marry a man that was so completely opposite everything she believed in. It wouldn't work. It hadn't worked with her mother and father so why did she think she could make it work with Alec? He was worse than her father! He was more powerful for starters. And power was bad. She didn't like people with a lot of power. They tended to walk all over everyone. This morning was a case in point, she thought angrily.

She didn't want to be a society wife, she thought, writing that down underneath "Controlling". "Irritating, obnoxious, inconsiderate" all made it to the list. She didn't have time to make a list of the people she wanted at her wedding because she was too busy making a list of all the reasons why they shouldn't get married. And that list encompassed all of Alec's personality flaws. She really didn't like the man right now. She wrote "manipulative" at the top and underlined it.

"Oooh!" she marched around the waiting room, thinking of other traits she hated in the man.

After several minutes of pacing, her fury dropped to a slow simmer. She was still going to get out of this wedding but at least now, she could think and make plans. She had to get her mother on her side as well. Once Elisia understood, then her father would definitely back her. She'd have to keep Alec away from her father though. Maybe there was some way she could limit the visitors in the hospital to only family members. Wasn't it supposed to be that way anyway?

She slipped into the hallway, about to question one of the nurses about that policy but saw Alec talking to one of the nurses and a doctor. Well, he wasn't actually talking. It was more of a commanding conversation. He seemed to be commanding and they were nodding their heads, almost pathetically eager to please him.

Well, that certainly put a damper on keeping him out. How was she going to tell the hospital staff that he wasn't allowed in her father's room when he was telling them what to do?

What a crazy situation she thought as she slouched down into yet another uncomfortable hospital chair, this one a teal blue that didn't match anything else in the waiting room.

This situation was all her fault so she only had herself to blame for her current predicament. If only she'd kept away from him. If only she'd had more self-discipline. If only... why couldn't she have fallen for some guy that was nice and artistic? More like her? They wouldn't get into fights. They wouldn't try to control each other but would respect each person's boundaries.

"What are you thinking about?" Alec asked, pulling her to her feet and directly into his arms while at the same time, taking the note pad away from her and tossing it onto the chair she'd just vacated.

He chuckled as he read through her list of grievances over her head. "This isn't exactly the best list for a wedding party."

"You manipulated me!" she grumbled against his chest, leaning her forehead against his shoulder and refusing to look up at him.

"Of course I did. You wouldn't agree to marry me this morning. I had to take things into my own hands."

Helen sighed and tried to pull out of his arms. "That's not a good start for a relationship, Alec."

"You're right. So tell me what kind of a wedding dress you'd like and I'll have it delivered. Your father is convinced he's going to be out of the hospital in two weeks and will be walking you down the aisle."

She pulled out of his arms, grateful that he gave her the little bit of space. "Alec, this is crazy. Our personalities simply won't work in a marriage," she tried to explain. "Look at my mother and father," she said, waving her hands in the direction of the elevator where her father was being wheeled to the private wing of the hospital.

Both of them glanced down the hallway just in time to see Elisia bend down and kiss her father affectionately on the mouth, then smooth back his hair, looking down at him with all her love shining through her eyes.

"Okay, well, not at this moment," she said with exasperation but also a large dose of relief and love for both of her parents. "But they are so opposite, they can't even live in the same country."

"They appear to have worked things out," he countered, leaning one shoulder against the doorway while he listened to her try and weasel out of their impending nuptials.

Helen shook her head and turned away. "Not really," she said. "They lived together for only a few years before they had to separate. Neither one of them ever remarried. I don't think my mother even dated another man."

"Indicates to me that they were made to live with each other. Why didn't they?"

"Because they were miserable living together. They fought all the time. My father wanted one life and my mother wanted something else. Their two personalities were too strong and they couldn't make it work."

"It will be different with us," he said firmly and with absolute certainty.

"How will you be able to accomplish that?" she asked in exasperation. "We can't even get along now. How do you think we'll learn to get along when we're around each other more often?"

"We don't always fight," he said, his eyes conveying his meaning.

"Not *that* way," she countered. "Besides, we can't have sex all the time."

"Says who?" He laughed at her blush but shook his head. "Helen, you're not getting out of this wedding so you might as well learn to accept it. We won't argue all the time. You'll learn to live with me and I'll compromise as well. It's that simple."

Helen couldn't help it, she actually burst out laughing at his suggestion. "Alec, when was the last time you compromised?"

He looked exasperated. "I've compromised."

"Uh, huh. Name one time that happened."

He thought for a moment. "I didn't drag you to bed the first night we were together."

Helen shook her head. "You didn't compromise on that. It just wasn't going to happen."

"Are you saying that I couldn't have convinced you to come back to my place if I'd really set my mind to it?"

Helen gulped, knowing that he probably could have tried. And she might not have been strong enough to stop him. "Name a time when there isn't sex involved."

He thought for a moment longer, then looked down at her. "I disagree with you wandering around London with your cell phone turned off. I hate your tiny apartment but I haven't moved you out of it. Yet," he said, spoiling the compromise. "I think you're too liberal in your politics, you drive me nuts about socializing with my staff but I've instituted a more lenient policy on some social gatherings."

Her eyes widened. "You did?"

"Yes. I don't like it, but Edna came back and thanked me for giving her the day off for her birthday."

"Why don't you like it? That's a very nice thing to do!" She knew by the look on his face that he wasn't thrilled with the concept.

"It isn't a formal day off, it's just a casual policy and I'm reserving that policy only for Edna and perhaps a few other staff members."

"And you will casually decide when to apply that policy," she guessed accurately and laughed when he only stared back at her, basically confirming her statement. Standing up, she patted him on his shoulder. "It's okay, Alec. That's progress. You're starting to show a human side to you. Be careful though," she chuckled, "your staff might take advantage of your leniency and work only twelve hour days instead of their normal fourteen."

"You think you're pretty funny, don't you," he said and pushed away from the wall against which he'd been leaning. He slowly closed the gap between them, trapping her against the wall on the opposite side of the hallway and leaning into her. "I have news for you, my dear. You're going to marry me in two weeks' time, and best of all, you're going to admit that you love me."

Helen didn't like the sound of that. It came too close to all of her fears. "I don't think so," she whispered and tried to inch away from him but he anticipated that and trapped her more effectively, pressing his legs and hips against her own. "Let me go, Alec." She said the words, but they were breathy and didn't sound very convincing.

He laughed at her efforts but moved away from her. "Despite the fact that I'd like to throw you over my shoulder and carry you back to my place, make love to you for the next twenty four hours, I'm going to give you the space you need." She started to say something but he interrupted, "Not too much space though. If I do you'll run away because you're terrified of what I make you feel."

"I'm not," she said indignantly, and was glad that the sound was louder this time.

He shook his head and looked down at her. "You are, but that's okay. I'll tell you something myself," he said and took her hand, leading her down the hospital hallway towards her father's new room, "I'm terrified myself."

Helen made an inappropriate sound as she rolled her eyes. "Right," she scoffed.

"I am. I'm terrified that you'll run away and I'll never see you again. I'm afraid you'll not love me nearly as much as I love you. I'm afraid I'll hurt you in some way that I won't realize and I'm afraid that you'll hear my next statement and be furious with me."

Helen was still too stunned by his second declaration. Her mind was reeling and she could barely concentrate on what he was saying, didn't realize that he had to pull her off to the side of the hospital hallway since she'd stopped walking and was blocking the other patients and visitors. Looking up at his handsome face, her heart swelled with amazement. "You're afraid I won't love you as much as you love me?" she whispered, her eyes watering.

He pulled her closer, his hand gently cupping the side of her face as he looked down into her now watery eyes and nodded. "Yes. I didn't think I'd ever find anyone quite like you but you barreled into my life, disrupting every moment of my routine, driving me absolutely nuts and making me want you more with every moment I spent in your company. I love the way you drive me crazy, I love the way you catch every moment of life as if it were precious, I love the way you bring strangers into your world and care for them as if they were family."

By this time, the tears had spilled over and were sliding down her cheeks. He smiled softly, the pad of his thumb wiping the tears away as he continued. "I love you, Helen. I love everything about you and I want you in my life, driving me so crazy I can barely think. Would you please do that for me?"

Helen couldn't help but laugh and shook her head, hiccupping as she absorbed all that he'd said. "That's so much better of a marriage proposal than simply telling me that we're going to be married."

He stood still, waiting. "Before you answer, you have to know something."

She didn't like the sound of that. "What?" she asked warily.

Alec looked around, then pulled her into an empty hospital room. "Your father's heart attack?" he waited until she'd nodded her head before continuing. "It wasn't brought on by anything you did. It was brought on by the fact that his company was in financial trouble and," he took a deep breath, "I came in and bought it up before he realized what had happened."

Helen just stood there for a long moment, staring at him as if he'd spoken in a foreign language.

Alec waited for the outburst, prepared to do just about anything to keep her, but unwilling to let her go. The stunned expression on her face wasn't what he'd been expecting though.

Helen turned away, walked towards the hospital bed, back to the door, and then back to the bed once again. Her mind was s whirling, taking in the facts, figuring out the details of the issues he hadn't told her. Finally, after several long moments, she looked up and noticed the tense shoulders that looked like he was bracing to be physically assaulted and the jaw that was clenching, ready for just about anything. Her heart melted just a little more and she sighed.

"You didn't know it was my father's company though, right?"

There was a brief pause, then he shook his head. "No. I didn't know. I never made the connection between your last names. That's one reason why I didn't say anything when I left you that first morning even though I wanted nothing more than to pull you back in my arms and forget about the world."

Helen thought back to that morning, about how grim his expression had been at the time. She'd been too devastated by her own worries to have considered what he might have gone through but now that she thought about it, she realized that he'd been pretty upset that morning. Not that a stranger would have noticed. Alec didn't really allow others to see his emotions. But she'd learned, she realized. And she'd grasped that something had been terribly wrong. And then her phone call had come in and she'd been too worried about her father to think about what Alec might have been going through. "You were upset when you'd gotten the news."

"Yes."

"And you didn't know. But could you make me a deal?" she asked, moving closer and smiling up at his face.

"Anything." He gently touched her arms as she stepped within his reach, seemingly afraid to be his normal brash, confident self and pull her closer.

Helen didn't like that he was tentative. She understood in that moment that his confidence, actually, his arrogance, was something she really liked about him. He took what he wanted but was considerate enough to step back when he needed to. But if he'd been any less confident and assertive, she never would have fallen in love with him. She needed a man who wasn't afraid of her, wasn't afraid to challenge her. She wouldn't win often, but he would definitely make life more interesting.

Alec watched carefully as her mind worked, her eyes darting all around, and he relaxed slightly when her gorgeous, sexy lips started to smile. It was small at first, but after several moments, her smile seemed to light up the room.

"Would you promise that the next company you take over, please talk to me first?"

Alec was so surprised by such an easy request he didn't react initially. When he finally grasped what she was asking, he threw back his head and laughed, pulling her into his arms and lifting her off her feet. "Absolutely," he said, kissing her deeply. "As long as you're naked and driving me crazy," he said before he kissed her once again.

Helen laughed, filled with joy and amazement that such an incredible man had stolen her heart. "I love you," she said and wrapped her arms around his neck, reveling in how wonderful he felt.

Epilogue

Helen peered into the church, her eyes hungrily seeking out the only important person. When she saw Alec standing at the front, her body tensed with anticipation. He was so incredibly handsome, she thought. His dark suit made him look so strong and wonderful. She couldn't tell if he was nervous or calm but then no one really knew how he was feeling.

And then he turned, his eyes catching hers and she just about jumped with the electric shock that went through her body. How could he have such a strong impact when he was so far away?

The music started and Helen pulled her eyes away, glancing at her father who was standing proud next to her. He had almost fully recovered, news of her wedding challenging him to follow the doctor's instructions carefully. It helped that Elisia had moved back into his life and was watching over him. The two of them were embarrassingly happy these days. With Alec taking over Petros's business while he recovered, Elisia was able to shower him with her love and show him that he could slow down and enjoy life. Helen could honestly say that, besides herself and Alec, she'd never seen two people more in love than her parents right now.

Which isn't to say that she and Alec were a match made in heaven. The man continuously tried to bully her into doing what he wanted. Just the other day, he ordered her father's housekeeper to move all of her clothes into his penthouse. Which would have been fine except he didn't bother to consult her about the change. So she'd simply moved her clothes back into her father's house. He'd been livid when he'd discovered what she'd done, arguing that they were to be married in a few days so what was the point of not moving now.

She smiled at the memory of how they'd ended that argument,

her body tightening in anticipation of more arguments in the future. Well, actually, they hadn't really ended the argument. Alec had just lifted her into his arms and kissed her, despite the fact that nothing had been resolved. It had ended quite nicely though. And afterwards, she asked him how he would feel if their daughter were to move into a man's home before the wedding and a hard, angry expression had come over his handsome features. His response was a simple nod, which she'd taken as acceptance that she'd made her point.

But now, looking at all the guests who were watching her cousins walk down the aisle, she shivered in excitement. She was going to become this powerful, dynamic man's wife! And he would be her husband, a joy settling into her heart when she accepted that she and Alec would have so many wonderful, amazing and frustrating days together.

When the music changed, her father stiffened and smiled at his daughter. "Are you ready?" he asked softly, pride showing through his teary expression.

"Very much so, Papa." She smiled as she hugged his arm.

When she was handed off to Alec, she almost laughed at his possessive expression. He thought he had won, but really, she'd won. This magnificent man was hers! She couldn't believe how much she loved him, despite all of his arrogance. Or maybe she loved him because of that attribute.

"I love you," she whispered up to him.

In response, he pulled her closer, his eyes showing her how much he loved her right back.

A message from Elizabeth:
This book was written when I was still working full time. Every night, I'd come home from my corporate job and, after my kids were in bed, I'd drag out my laptop and start writing. It was the perfect way to end my stressful day! I hope that you enjoyed this story and, if you wouldn't mind, could you leave a review? Just go back to the retailer's book page – and I thank you!

As usual, if you don't want to leave feedback in a public forum, feel free to e-mail me directly at elizabeth@elizabethlennox.com. I answer all e-mails personally, although it sometimes takes me a while. Please don't be offended if I don't respond immediately. I tend to lose myself in writing stories and have a hard time pulling my head out of the book.

Elizabeth

Want to read a short excerpt from another stand alone book? Keep scrolling!

Excerpt from "The Duke's Willful Wife"
Now Available!

Sasha picked up the paintbrush, her fingers shaking and her stomach churning with fear and anticipation. "I'm over him," she whispered out loud, ignoring the cold mist that showed her breath as she took the step closer to the canvas. Dipping her brush into the first color, she braced herself and started the process, the first colors hitting the white canvas no longer a shock to her mind but still something she didn't particularly enjoy. But since this whole process of painting this particular subject was physically painful for her, she ignored the starting sensation and concentrated on working through to get to the answer.

There was no other way to do it, she told herself, but to dive right in and face the results. Being afraid of the answer wasn't going to solve the problem and she wouldn't know the truth until she started. Procrastinating wouldn't give her the information she desperately needed.

Impatiently, she pushed her long, brown hair out of her way, tucking it up on top of her head with the end of her paint brush, uncaring that a bit of paint smeared across her high cheekbone. She wore no makeup, but her soft, brown eyes and peaches and cream complexion were rarely viewed by anyone anymore. She went out each day for a long walk and she occasionally saw the others in the village, but the only daily care she took in her appearance was to remove the paint smock that covered her from neck to knee while she worked. She was unaware, and unconcerned if people questioned her appearance.

At least that had been the case over the past year.

Classical music flowed around her as she worked on the painting. She didn't stop for food, didn't notice the light changing as the morning turned to afternoon, nor when the evening faded into night, and neither did she acknowledge the ache in her legs from standing all day. It was almost midnight before she put her paintbrush down and sighed in frustration.

As she looked at the painting, her heart lurched, the truth staring at her from the eyes she'd just painted. The truth was irrevocable and no matter how many times she told herself that she didn't, when she painted his face, she knew she was still in love with her husband.

She sighed with the acceptance that she wasn't yet over the man who had hurt her so deeply that even a year later, she still felt as if a hole had been torn out of her chest. Maintaining a stoic face while she worked, Sasha carefully cleaned her brushes and set them in the appropriate place in their holders to dry out, meticulously ensuring that they were immaculate and ready for her next project.

When she was finished with her supplies, she wearily carried the canvas to the barn behind her tiny cottage and stored it with the others that she'd worked on recently. The paintings here were items she'd either started and hadn't finished because she'd lost the inspiration, or that she didn't want the world to see because they were too personal or not good enough. This one fell into all of those categories so she stacked it towards the back, pulling the heavy tarp over the stack to ensure dust and water didn't get to it, and made sure that the moth balls were in place to deter some of the more curious animals from damaging any of the pieces. She might not be ready to sell or get rid of these efforts, but that didn't mean she wanted anything to happen to them.

Back in her cottage, she turned off the music, poured herself a glass of milk for dinner, then climbed into bed without bothering to change. Worn out jeans, flannel, tattered shirt and all, she just needed the warmth of the relative softness of her bed. And the pillows. She pulled them close, hugging one to her chest and the other tucked under her head.

This softness wasn't the same because the pillows didn't emanate the same heat as his arms and chest and they were much too soft compared to his muscles that were more analogous to rocks than anything else, but close enough and they were all she had at the moment, she thought as the tears spilled down her cheeks.

Tomorrow would be better, she promised herself. And she wouldn't try again for another month. Long walks, maybe some different music and a new painting. Her mind went through all the rituals she'd discovered that would help her get through the day. One breath at a time, she sighed into the night. Just one breath, one moment, one step at a time.

The following morning, she forced herself to fix some breakfast and eat it. It was only a soft boiled egg and whole wheat toast, but it was more than she'd eaten the whole previous day. A cup of tea warmed her up and she pulled her sneakers on for her morning walk. She pushed herself harder this time, walking around the pond, through the village, smiling and waving to the people she saw. She'd grown up in this small town so she knew just about everyone, but she didn't socialize a great deal anymore. Ever since Dante and his accusations, his rejection of her, she hadn't felt strong enough to be around other people.

Soon though, she'd start accepting some of the invitations. She needed to get out more, to be with other people and stop acting like a miserable, old recluse. Her activities lately weren't healthy and she needed to rejoin the world, to feel life again even if it might be painful at times. She knew she wasn't ready to start dating again, but she needed to reconnect with her friends, especially her college friends. She missed Kallista and Dana terribly and she knew they worried about her. She e-mailed with them when she remembered to log into her account, but the communication was sporadic. Dana was married with a baby on the way and Kallista was doing well as a journalist. They both had stopped by over the past year to check in on her and she'd done a relatively good job of convincing them that she was okay.

The banging on the door as she stepped through her back access startled her. Since the house was so small, she could see straight through from the back to her front entrance but the solid oak wouldn't allow her to see through and discover who had invaded her space so unexpectedly.

"Sasha! I'm here for the paintings. I know you're here so don't try and pretend otherwise," the male voice said.

Sasha's body relaxed as she released a relieved laugh, then hurried to the front door. "Robert, you know I'd never pretend with you," she said and hugged him enthusiastically. "What are you doing way out here in the country? I told you I'd bring the paintings to you Monday and I know you abhor leaving your precious city life and risk running into a leaf or, heaven forbid, a bug."

Sasha's agent and friend stepped through the front door and took his favorite client into his arms, as much to greet her as to determine if she was taking care of herself. As his arms closed around her slender frame, he became worried that she wasn't eating well.

"I didn't trust you to be on time and you know that's a completely justified terror when it comes to you lately. Your sense of timeliness seems to have disappeared completely. Besides, Monday is too far in the future. I need the paintings this weekend."

He surveyed her face, noting the more pronounced cheekbones and prominent, brown eyes still filled with so much loneliness. Damn that man who had done this to her gentle soul! Sasha was one of those sweet, caring people who pushed spiders out of her house instead of stomping on them. How Dante Fuitello could do this to such a beautiful woman was beyond anything Robert could understand.

Sasha pulled away, knowing that Robert would comment on her weight if he felt how much she'd lost in the past few weeks. And since there wasn't a whole lot to lose in the first place, he wouldn't be shy about mentioning her health, a subject that he brought up constantly it seemed.

"I thought you had a full gallery." She pulled him into her house, excited to see him but not sure why he'd come all this way instead of waiting for her to deliver the paintings she'd promised. His comment about being too slow was worrisome, only compounded by the fact that Robert was a city man, completely in tune with the rhythm of London and all the excitement available. He hated coming out to the country where she lived, considering it too "earthy".

"I did until I sold your last two yesterday." He looked around the dark, dingy little cottage that had only four rooms, a number that was abhorrently tiny in his estimation. "You're a wealthy woman and a famous artist now. Why are you still living in this hovel?"

Sasha rolled her eyes at the comment he made about her humble dwelling each time he visited, horrified that anyone would live in a place that doesn't have hardwood floors and twelve foot ceilings with strategically designed lighting to enhance one's living space.

"I love this hovel. Thank you very much for not disrespecting the hovel." She moved into the galley style kitchen that was about the size of some people's closet and put her battered tea kettle on one of the two burners of her ancient stove. With a flick of the lighter, a flame popped up under the kettle.

Robert leaned against the rough, wooden door frame that looked like a termite had rejected it about a hundred years ago.

"The condo next to mine is about to go on the market. I can tell my neighbor that you're interested. Lots of light, plenty of room and it doesn't smell like turpentine or burnt toast all the time." He looked around disdainfully. "How in the world do you create such amazing masterpieces in this kind of light?"

Sasha looked away, the memory of the most amazing place she'd ever painted coming to mind. This little cottage was the antithesis of that room with all the windows and natural light, the skylights that let in the sunshine no matter what time of the day.

Unfortunately, with that wonderful room came a not-so-perfect existence. One she had tried, and failed, to endure. "This place is perfect for me. At least for now." She still held out the hope that she'd get over that time in her life and be able to move on.

To stop Robert from commenting on her home, she changed the subject. "I only have three pictures ready for you unfortunately."

Robert rolled his eyes. "Do you have any life outside of painting?" he asked without sarcasm. For an artist of her caliber to produce three paintings in the last month, he suspected that she barely slept and did nothing other than paint. He also knew that painting was her way of working through her emotions, which had been severely tattered, but maybe if she got out a bit, she might recover more quickly. And for him to want an artist to slow down, which would mean less commissions for his bank account, that was genuine concern as Robert never really considered himself very selfless. But if she didn't slow down, she was going to burn out and that also wouldn't be good, for his bank account or his friendship with a woman who was truly special to him.

Sasha looked up at him, distressed by his comment. "Am I too slow? I'm sorry...." She started to say but Robert interrupted her with a laugh.

"Dear, three paintings from you is like money in the bank. I don't know any other artist who can produce like you can so please, ignore my silly comments and understand that I'm absolutely thrilled with three paintings from you. I have some artists that work on one painting a year, and they don't have half as much talent as you do. With all the emotion you put into your paintings, I don't know how you get through the day. Your productivity concerns me, is all."

Sasha was relieved, not sure what the art world expected of her. It wouldn't have mattered anyway. She could only paint what she felt at the speed at which she was feeling things. The past year had been a pretty emotional disaster for her so she'd been extremely prolific lately. But she hoped to be able to focus on only one painting per year at some point. Maybe when she wasn't so centered on the past, she could....

Someday, she reassured herself. There will come a point in her life when she wouldn't feel this kind of pain or betrayal.

There had been joy at one point. That period in her work had been a completely different style, but it had lasted for only a short period of time. She knew others who viewed her work might see the emotions in her paintings, but she hoped that they didn't understand them. Not completely at least.

An hour later, she helped Robert carefully pack the paintings into his trunk, ensuring that they were cautiously stored so they wouldn't be damaged, then waved goodbye to him as he drove back down the dusty, gravel road that was her driveway. He'd made her laugh this afternoon, which was a good thing. He was a delightful friend, even though she knew his motivation was more than a little mercenary. Robert gathered friends only to further his art business. Everyone had a purpose, either on the supply or demand side of the chain and he treated each person accordingly.

Sasha knew this about him and still accepted his friendship, but was also relieved when he drove away after each visit, needing his interruptions but appreciating the stillness and peace of her hideaway even more after he'd left.

Back inside, she put the kettle on to heat more water, her mind considering options for what she might paint next. Thoughts flitted through her mind and she considered and rejected some of them, storing others away. She was just about to pick up her sketch pad to work through some ideas when a strange noise in the distance distracted her. Glancing at the clock, she realized it was later than she thought. She hadn't had lunch yet and it was already three o'clock in the afternoon.

Placing her sketch pad back on the table, she told herself she'd take just a peek outside to find out what the odd sound that was breaking the stillness of the early springtime afternoon. Then she'd make a sandwich and maybe even venture into the village to grab a cup of coffee, talk to some of her old friends a bit and make sure she stretched her social skills slightly.

The noise was becoming louder and she tucked her sketch pad down between the overstuffed chair and her easel, glancing out the window.

What she saw made her heart stop for a split second. Then her stomach dropped, followed immediately by the painful racing of her heart.

A helicopter?

There was only one reason a helicopter would be heading this way. The town was too quiet, too isolated for any other reason.

Sure enough, a moment later, the helicopter hovered over the small field in front of her cottage, then slowly descended. Glancing around the tree line of her property, she noted there were already several men standing around the edge of her field, the bulges under their dark suits barely concealing the large weapons Sasha knew to be hidden underneath the deceptive material.

As soon as the helicopter touched down, she watched in horror as the one man she'd prayed never to see again outside of a white fabric canvas stepped out, his long legs eating up the space between the powerful machine and her tiny, dilapidated cottage.

He wore expensive sunglasses and a perfectly tailored, summer weight tan suit with a white shirt opened at the collar, but nothing could hide the power of this man. It was physically apparent both in the way he walked and the commanding way he approached the world and her house, not to mention the muscles that were ripped over his body from grueling daily workouts that a lesser man would collapse under. No suit could hide the power of that physique, she thought while her mind whirled frantically.

As he approached her door with that intimidating stride, she wasn't sure what to do. To let him into her house would mean that his whole personality would invade the private space she'd created, a space that was devoid of any memories of this man. To not let him in would also be dangerous. Not that he would allow that though. When Dante Fuitello wanted in, everyone else needed to just step back. She'd never known him to let anyone stand in his way. Sasha had no idea what the consequences would be if someone dared to challenge him, because it simply was never done. At least she'd never seen or heard of it happening.

And then he was there, standing in front of her house. The option of not letting him inside was gone and her whole body trembled with memories of their time together, of how passionate and wonderful he could be.

As well as how brutally cold, impersonal and dispassionate he could turn. She'd experienced both sides and never wanted either extreme again.

Her life was calm and, if not peaceful, at least it wasn't disrupted by the angry words and horrible accusations that had been almost daily life with him. And the passion, she thought. Yes, there had been more passion than she'd thought was possible. Dante could bring her to the heights of heaven, but life with him could also be a living hell. Loving him was....difficult.

The knock on the door was fast and reflected the confidence this man had that the world would react exactly as he demanded it would, and it didn't matter if it was the stock market or a company, somehow the world complied and bowed to this man's wishes.

She couldn't open the door. So many feelings were clogging her senses right now that her feet were rooted on the floor. There were no messages from her brain to her feet telling her to move. She simply stood in the middle of her small den, staring at the door.

Sasha should have known that he'd just enter. Dante wasn't the kind of man who waited for permission so when the initial knock didn't provide the desired reaction, he simply opened the door and walked in.

Why hadn't she locked the door? Why hadn't she hidden in her bedroom? Why hadn't she run into the woods at the very first realization of a helicopter approaching?

As he stepped into her house, he had to duck underneath the door frame because he was so tall. The house had been made over two hundred years ago at a time when people were shorter, but even by today's standards Dante was huge. At six feet, three inches tall, he was at least half a head taller than most men. If that didn't separate him out from the rest of the world, his black hair and black eyes, chiseled facial features that were normally devoid of any emotion except for the rare moments when he was mildly amused, would capture anyone's attention.

After they'd stood there watching each other for a long, awkward moment, she finally asked, "What are you doing here?"

Dante took in the one woman who had gotten beneath his guard. The one person who had never bowed to his bidding, never reacted the way he expected. He was surprised at how angry he had become just by entering her world. He'd thought this would be a simple mission but seeing her standing in front of him, looking like the goddess he'd first glimpsed so long ago, his reaction was probably understandable.

She'd lost a good deal of weight over the past year. She'd always been thin but now her jeans hung on her hips and the large shirt that was tied at her waist couldn't cinch in enough. It was a man's shirt anyway and on her delicate frame, it was about ten sizes too large.

Eyes that had once danced with laughter and excitement over everything, were now large, brown saucers in a face that looked....haunted. She was pale, the only color in her face were those still beautiful, soulful, brown eyes. And he had no idea what she'd done with her hair. He suspected nothing at all which was a crime since this woman's hair had been the softest, most luxurious thing he'd ever....

Dante forced his mind back to the problem. "I tried calling you," he said to break the silence.

Sasha wasn't sure how to respond. When she worked, she shut off her cell phone so if he'd tried to reach her, he would have gotten her voice mail and she hadn't checked it yet. She tried to speak, but the words were stuck in her throat. She coughed and tore her hungry eyes away from him. "Would you like some tea?" she asked, manners coming to save her in this instance. She wasn't sure what was the polite comment to make when one's estranged husband walked through the door unexpectedly.

There was no answer but she didn't care. Sasha moved into her tiny kitchen, needing to do something with her hands. She filled up the kettle and lit the burner, becoming more nervous as he prowled her cottage, looking at all the details. There wasn't much to see. The furniture was sparse with only one large chair and an ottoman for reading, a side table and lamp, all of which were positioned for a body to obtain maximum heat from the now cold and blackened fireplace. There was an old, wooden bookshelf filled with various genres, but that was about it. Her dining room had been converted to her studio and that contained several lights to help her work, stacks of varying sized canvases, her easel and paints. There wasn't a table and no chairs. The two windows and another fireplace were on the opposite wall, but the room wasn't meant for guests, although he prowled through that space as well but didn't seem very interested, only mildly curious.

Sasha pulled down two cups and fiddled with the bags of tea, busying herself until she got up the nerve to ask him why he had decided to break away from his business empire to visit her quaint little town. While they'd been married, the man had worked fourteen to eighteen hour days, sometimes seven days a week. He'd rarely taken the time to spend quiet days with her. At least that was the case when they'd returned to his home in Rome.

The whole time he prowled her domain, she tried to work through in her mind why he was here. There had been no communication between the two of them, and even though she'd been expecting notice, she hadn't received anything from him or his lawyers asking for a divorce. Taking a deep breath, she stepped out from her hiding place and faced him, her chin going up defiantly.

"Why did you come here?" she asked, angry that her voice quivered slightly, revealing how emotionally distraught she was with his presence.

"Aren't you happy to see me?" he asked, his voice dripping with sarcasm.

"After the accusations you tossed at me the last time we were together, I'd rather hoped never to see you again."

"After the perfidy I discovered about you, I had resolved that very same thing."

"What you *think* you discovered," she corrected quickly. "You're too distrusting to know what you saw."

She snapped her mouth shut quickly. The last time they'd had this argument she'd sworn she would never defend herself against his callous words again. There was just something about this man that made her furious and defensive.

He shrugged slightly. "I'm not going to rehash the same, tedious argument with you, Sasha."

She was relieved, because this wasn't a dispute she could win and maintain her word to a friend.

"Good. Then tell me why you're here and get out of my house." In her fantasy world, she lifted him up and tossed him out, just like she felt he'd done to her. He'd never touched her in anger, but his words had hurt just as badly.

"Nonna is ill."

There wasn't much he could have said that would have broken through her pain and anger at their last parting, but those words got her attention. During the nightmarish year that she'd been with this amazing man, his Grandmother Rennata, Nonna, had been the one steady, friendly and loving force in her life. She'd been a true friend and confidant.

"She's not!"

He didn't even blink at her vehement rejection, but continued to stare at her steadily. "She's in the intensive care unit. She fell sick last week, but refused to see a doctor. It became steadily worse until two days ago when she didn't come down for dinner. When my mother went upstairs to check on her, Nonna Rennata couldn't be revived. We called an ambulance and by the time the doctors examined her, they explained that she'd had a series of heart attacks."

Those two last words spoken about the small, wonderful woman who had taken Sasha under her wing and treated her like a granddaughter struck her as painful. "No!"

Dante realized that his wife was genuinely upset by this, which confused him. She'd always kept apart from the family. He had no idea that Sasha cared one whit about his grandmother even though the elderly lady had asked for Sasha repeatedly during her illness.

"She's stable," he said quickly, but the pained expression in his wife's eyes didn't diminish.

When Sasha thought she could speak without her voice breaking, she asked, "How long has she been in the hospital?

"Three days."

With a slight nod, Sasha accepted this, berating herself for not already knowing and keeping in touch with Rennata more closely. They communicated via e-mail and text, but the communication was sporadic and Sasha only logged into her e-mail about once a week. "Is she still...?"

Dante's mouth compressed in frustration and confusion. "As I said, she's stable. But she's been asking for you."

That snapped Sasha out of her panic and gave her something to do, something to help. "Of course. If Nonna needs me, I'll be there as fast as I can." She was already walking towards the stairs to pack a bag.

"We can be airborne as soon as you grab your purse."

Made in United States
North Haven, CT
03 April 2024

50877192R00065